REA
ALLEN COUNTY PUBLIC LIBRARY
3 1833 02328
P9-EEI-706
Fiction
Hazard, Barbara.
Dangerous deceits

an-

a's

mount and sent her tumbling. It was even worse that he showed no remorse after determining Diana had suffered no serious harm. In fact, the look in his eyes instantly shifted from proper concern to quite improper pleasure.

"Surely you understand my position at the moment is most unseemly," she reproved him with anger.

He grinned down at her, lying there on the grassy verge with the skirts of her habit disarranged. "On the contrary, I find your position provocative," he told her. "Most provocative. Come tell me your name."

Diana shook her head firmly. "I do not talk to rakes, sir. And you are one, aren't you?"

As he took her in his arms, she knew how right she was about him. And as she felt his kiss, she began to suspect how wrong she was about herself. . . .

SIGNET REGENCY ROMANCE

Coming in October 1995

Carla Kelly
Reforming Lord Ragsdale

Karen Harbaugh
The Vampire Viscount

Patricia Oliver
An Immodest Proposal

1-800-253-8476
ORDER DIRECTLY
WITH VISA OR MASTERCARD

Dangerous Deceits

by

Barbara Hazard

A SIGNET BOOK

Allen County Public Library
900 Webster Street
PO Box 2270
Fort Wayne, IN 46801-2270

SIGNET
Published by the Penguin Group
Penguin Books USA Inc., 375 Hudson Street,
New York, New York 10014, U.S.A.
Penguin Books Ltd, 27 Wrights Lane,
London W8 5TZ, England
Penguin Books Australia Ltd, Ringwood,
Victoria, Australia
Penguin Books Canada Ltd, 10 Alcorn Avenue,
Toronto, Ontario, Canada M4V 3B2
Penguin Books (N.Z.) Ltd, 182-190 Wairau Road,
Auckland 10, New Zealand

Penguin Books Ltd, Registered Offices:
Harmondsworth, Middlesex, England

First published by Signet, an imprint of Dutton Signet,
a division of Penguin Books USA Inc.

First Printing, September, 1995
10 9 8 7 6 5 4 3 2 1

Copyright © B. W. Hazard, Ltd., 1995
All rights reserved

REGISTERED TRADEMARK—MARCA REGISTRADA

Printed in the United States of America

Without limiting the rights under copyright reserved above, no part of this publication may be reproduced, stored in or introduced into a retrieval system, or transmitted, in any form, or by any means (electronic, mechanical, photocopying, recording, or otherwise), without the prior written permission of both the copyright owner and the above publisher of this book.

BOOKS ARE AVAILABLE AT QUANTITY DISCOUNTS WHEN USED TO PROMOTE PRODUCTS OR SERVICES. FOR INFORMATION PLEASE WRITE TO PREMIUM MARKETING DIVISION, PENGUIN BOOKS USA INC., 375 HUDSON STREET, NEW YORK, NY 10014.

If you purchased this book without a cover you should be aware that this book is stolen property. It was reported as "unsold and destroyed" to the publisher and neither the author nor the publisher has received any payment for this "stripped book."

Dear Reader,

Generally, when I finish a book, it is as complete as I can make it. But sometimes, the story and characters linger in my mind. *Dangerous Deceits* is one of those books. It was my seventh Regency, published in 1982. I was pleased with it then, but over the years I've always wanted to improve it. Make it funnier, for one thing, for although the deceits in the story are dangerous to the hero and heroine's future together, they're also amusing. And besides the comedy, I wanted to make the duke and Diana come alive—give them a more endearing love story.

I hope you'll enjoy the new version of one of my old favorites.

1

On a clear October morning in the year 1814, Miss Diana Travis stood quietly to one side of the altar in the village church in Eastham, and watched her older sister Anne repeat her wedding vows as she became the bride of Reginald Warren, Viscount Stafford. Diana thought Anne looked lovely in her gown of white silk, the veiling on her matching bonnet half hiding her dark brown curls and rosy cheeks, now blushing with happiness and delight. Diana wondered how she would look as a bride when it was her turn to marry. She was sure of one thing, though. She would be vastly different.

With her midnight-black hair that refused to curl no matter how long the papers or the tongs were applied, and her pale, creamy complexion that turned a golden tan whenever she forgot to wear a hat, she did not look at all like her sister. Instead of Anne's blue eyes, hers were a deep hazel, widely set and darkly lashed, and her generous mouth was most unlike Anne's sweet, pouting lips. Then too, where Anne was plump and rounded, Miss Diana was lithe and slim. She sighed a little as she bowed her head obediently in prayer. It seemed very hard to be so plain, for even at seventeen she knew she would never be the beauty Anne was. Sometimes, she wished fate had been kinder to her, and divided up the good looks between the two more equitably.

For her sister's wedding, she was wearing a new gown of pale yellow silk trimmed with lace, and she carried a bouquet of yellow and white chrysanthemums with a matching cluster in her hair. Her mother, in some despair, had finally allowed her to wear her hair up in a chignon for the occasion, and Diana had no idea how it enhanced her oval face and made her eyes seem larger and more mysterious. Nor did she have any idea how the color of her gown became her, so that many a gentleman whose glances might have been reserved for her sister before this, now found his eyes going again and again to the straight young figure of her bridesmaid, and wondering why he had never noticed how attractive the younger Travis daughter was.

Now Reggie was speaking in response to the vicar's prodding. Diana hoped he would get through his replies without a slip, for he had a tendency to stammer when he was excited or embarrassed. She saw Anne encouraging him with a warm smile, and how his color rose when he looked down at her. Lord Stafford was some seven years his bride's senior, but he still seemed young to Diana, even though he was turned twenty-six. When Anne had rushed to her sister's room to announce Reggie was even then speaking to their father and asking her hand in marriage, Diana had had to stifle an impulse to ask her if she really wanted to marry him. For herself, she thought him uninteresting—foppish and somewhat silly, with little conversation or wit. But she had repressed these traitorous thoughts when she saw how happy her sister was. Later she had asked her mother about it in the privacy of her boudoir where she had found her writing letters.

Mrs. Travis had put down her quill to give her younger daughter a long, level look.

"You must remember, my dear, you are not Anne. Where you would be miserable with Stafford, she will be supremely happy."

"How can you be sure, Mama?"

Mrs. Travis had chuckled a little. "I have seen you looking at him these past weeks; such an incredulous look, too! You do not admire him—he is neither quick nor learned nor witty; attributes you, my dear, have in abundance."

Diana's eyes had widened. "I *do*?" she asked in wonder, for her mother was not given to fulsome compliments.

Mrs. Travis nodded and reached up to pat her cheek. "Indeed you do, dear Di, but for all of that, your sister will be content with her husband. You'll see."

At that she had turned back to her letters again, leaving her daughter to ponder what she had said; in effect, that Anne was not quick nor learned nor witty, either. Diana had to admit, much as she loved her sister, her mother was right. Where she was always reading in her spare time, Anne was gossiping with her friends, flirting with the neighborhood beaux, or engrossed in planning new gowns. And where Diana liked nothing better than a heady conversation with her father about some current event or a new book they had both just read, Anne would quickly excuse herself and leave them to help her mother with some task in the stillroom, or to do some needlework.

Well, Diana thought now as the vicar announced the benediction, Mama is probably right. She looks happy in any case, and Reggie appears to be completely besotted.

As the wedding party left the church to the huzzahs

and applause of the assembled villagers, Diana looked up suddenly, for some reason feeling slightly uneasy. She noticed her sister was also looking to where a gentleman on horseback had paused in the road to observe the wedding party. He raised his hat and bowed over the saddle in tribute to the bride, and Anne's blushes grew even more rosy as she lowered her eyes in confusion. The gentleman turned aside to say something to his companion, and Diana continued to stare at him, for she had never seen anyone remotely like him in her entire life.

It was apparent he was above medium height, even though he was mounted, and he had the broadest shoulders and most powerful physique Diana had ever seen. One strong hand held his restless horse easily, but it was his face that attracted her. It was clean-shaven and she had the impression of a powerful nose, lean cheeks, a strong jaw, and a pair of disturbing eyes. She supposed he was handsome, but that was not the first thing anyone would think of. Rather, it was the aura of raw power and iron control he portrayed. She shivered a little.

As if aware of her fascinated gaze, now he glanced toward Diana, and those disturbing eyes narrowed in intent. She knew her face had paled, and she knew she ought to look away, but still their glances remained locked. Diana felt a helpless prisoner.

Suddenly he seemed to recall himself, and he bowed again, more deeply this time, to her alone. And still she stared at him, her hand tightening on her flowers until she felt the stems snap.

"For heaven's sake, stop staring, Di," her mother whispered from behind her, giving her a little push as Anne and her new husband went down the steps. "It is only two of Lord Barrett's guests. You must have heard he was having some gentlemen for the hunting. And here you stand, looking just like poor little Molly Parsons, gawking at the men with your mouth open, and she not right in the head. Come along now, do!"

Obediently, Diana lowered her eyes, stooping to adjust her sister's train as she started toward the carriage on Stafford's arm. In doing so, she missed the last, speculative look the stranger gave her before he rode away with his companion.

She had forgotten all about Lord Barrett's annual hunting party, for there was no traffic between his estate and Crompton Abbey, the Travis's home. Mr. Travis did not care for Lord Barrett and his friends. There had been a time when Anne and Diana would sit for hours, peeking through the hedge that separated their properties, and speculate on the wickedness that had prompted this rift, in their innocence devising all manner of foul deeds and extravagances. It was true Lord Barrett was seldom in residence, for he preferred the livelier life in London, but he never failed to put in an appearance during the hunting season, at which time the Travis sisters were more closely confined to the Abbey. Mrs. Travis shared her husband's views, not only about their neighbor but about the guests he was sure to entertain. She wanted no London rakes to catch sight of the innocent beauties who resided next door. It was a vast disappointment to both sisters that neither one of them had ever seen a rake, for surely he must be very, very wicked, and therefore, fascinating.

A festive meal had been prepared for the guests at the Abbey, and an orchestra engaged for dancing. Diana was surprised at all the attention that was paid to her. She had not thought to have so much enjoyment. But as she whirled down the floor with Sir Thomas Redding who had never so much as glanced her way before, and listened to his extravagant compliments, she was sure he had had too much champagne. Her thoughts went often to the stranger by the church gate, and she could not help comparing him to these gentlemen she had known all her life who were now begging for the honor of a dance. She thought it was almost as if his attention had caused the others to notice her, until she scolded herself for being fanciful.

Mrs. Travis, accepting the compliments of her friends on her daughter Anne's excellent match, nodded her head a little as she caught sight of Diana. She noticed she had attracted the attention of a Mr. Waitsfield, a wealthy bachelor, and she smiled to herself.

"You have every reason to look pleased, Sarah," her aunt, Lady Michaels, remarked as she accepted another glass of negus from her long-suffering companion. "A most gratifying match for Anne, and how Diana has come on! Such dignity and presence in one so young—remarkable! Keep her hair up like that. It becomes 'er. And, I wager, it will not be long before we are all summoned to the Abbey again to celebrate yet another happy occasion."

Mrs. Travis nodded tranquilly, although she found her Aunt Emma's comments a trifle strong and to the point. But then, when had they ever not been?

"Diana is but seventeen. Her father and I would be sorry to have her leave us just yet," she remarked.

"Nonsense! The sooner the better. Do you plan to take her to London later this month? She's ripe for the ton."

Sarah Travis sighed a little and wished her aunt's voice was not quite so loud and piercing and that at some point in her long life, she had learned to control her impulse to say the first thing that came into her head.

"I think not. Perhaps in the spring when she is eighteen. At the moment, her father and I do not consider her to be, er, ready."

Lady Michaels cackled. "You're thinkin' of her figger. But there are other ways a gel can be ready, you know, and unless I miss my guess, Miss Diana is right on the edge. Gels are like vegetables, Sarah—they sprout, grow, ripen, and get picked!"

As she laughed heartily at her own wit, Mrs. Travis wished she would forget the word "ripe." Or perhaps she could learn to compare Diana to a flower? The way she was talking, the girl sounded like a turnip.

Lady Michaels poked her with a bony finger. "Just see how she is captivating the gentlemen. Unless you take care, niece, you'll find her in love with some hearty farmer, and that would never do. It might have for Anne, maybe; not for Diana."

Silently, Sarah Travis agreed an Eastham squire was the last match she wanted for her younger daughter. She excused herself so she might see to her other guests, and as she went away, Lady Michaels nodded wisely and poked her companion in the ribs with her fan.

"Mark my words, Polly, Miss Diana is going to be a handful for someone, and soon. She'll not go meekly to the altar murmuring 'Yes, m'lord.' Remember her temper?"

Her companion, a poor distant cousin, nodded, but before she could comment Lady Michaels went on, "I hope Sarah will bring her to London so I can see the fun when the fireworks go off. Polly! I feel a draft—go find out where it is coming from at once. 'Tis all you're good for. Heaven knows you have no conversation."

Later Diana stood with her parents as the new bride and groom drove away in their carriage. They were to travel to one of the viscount's properties in Scotland, and then to his estate near Cuckfield. Diana did not expect to see them until Christmas and she felt a little sad. For although she and her sister were not at all alike, they had been constant companions, and Anne's cheerful nature and sunny smile had more than once coaxed Diana from a spell of low spirits, a state she succumbed to whenever she was bored or depressed.

Life at the Abbey once again settled into its normal pattern when the last of the wedding guests took their leave, and Diana told her mother one morning at breakfast she intended to go for a long ride.

Mrs. Travis frowned and she was surprised until the sound of a hunting horn came faintly to her ears.

"I had forgotten the hunt and Lord Barrett, Mama," she said.

Her father joined the conversation. "Be assured your mother has not, my dear. And I agree with her, since you refuse to take a groom. M'lord is entertaining a large party this year, and I do not wish you to run the risk of attracting their attention. Corinthians! Here-and-thereians—bah! You will remain on the Abbey grounds until they have left the neighborhood."

Diana agreed, but for the first time she felt a stab of resentment and rebellion. Surely her father was being unreasonable. After all, the men who visited Lord Barrett were all of the haut ton. She could not believe she would come to any harm at their hands for she was not some pretty dairymaid! Suddenly she recalled the man who had bowed to her outside the church, and she amended her thoughts. She could well believe she might come to some harm at *his* hands for he had looked more than capable of it if so he chose. Her mother interrupted her musings by asking her the condition of her best winter cloak, and she put the gentleman from her mind. It was somehow depressing to realize that she did not have to worry about the dangerous stranger for she would, in all probability, never see him again.

It was another week before Mr. Travis heard from his neighbor, Squire Beals, that the hunting party had left for town. He also heard several stories of their stay which he did not relate to his wife and daughter, for his lips had tightened in disgust at the telling.

Diana was quick to order her mare brought around early the next morning. She had been feeling pent-up—restless, riding only on the Abbey grounds, extensive though they were.

It was a crisp morning in early November and there was a touch of frost whitening the ground when Diana turned the mare's head down the drive. The mare was frisky in the cold air, and for a while it was all Diana could do to hold her in check. When she reached the first field, she turned in at an open gate, thinking a quick gallop would shake the fidgets out of Belle.

As the morning wore on, the sun warmed the ground and all trace of frost disappeared. It seemed almost a day in early autumn, and Diana began to feel uncomfortable in the heavy habit she had donned that morning when she could see her breath. She halted the mare in a quiet lane lined with hedges, and Belle pawed the ground impatiently.

"Behave yourself," Diana ordered as she loosened the stiff heavy collar of her habit. Suddenly she heard galloping hooves, but before she could react and grab the reins again to guide the mare to one side, a horse and rider thundered around the bend. It was much too fast a pace for such a winding lane with so many blind corners, and although the rider drew his mount up and away so sharply it reared, its hooves struck Belle lightly on the flank, and she tried to bolt.

"Steady, Belle, steady!" Diana cried as the mare bucked and tried to escape. Then she found herself falling from her sidesaddle to the dusty lane. She struck her head on a stone but she was not aware of it for she was concentrating on rolling to one side as fast as she could, to avoid those flashing hooves. In a moment, the danger was over, for before her eyes closed in relief, she saw the stranger from the church gate grasping Belle's bridle in an iron hand. She marveled at his strength, even as he dismounted to tie both horses to a nearby branch. Diana kept her eyes closed when she heard his hasty footsteps coming toward her.

"You little fool! I might have run you down," he muttered in a harsh, deep voice as he knelt beside her. Diana put one hand to her head. It was beginning to throb unpleasantly but she forgot it when she felt his hands going over her. She knew she should protest such an intimacy, but somehow it seemed easier to just lie still with her eyes closed while she tried to catch her breath.

"Can you move? There are no broken bones that I can discover, but tell me if you are in pain," his quick, harsh voice asked. He shook her a little and her eyes flew open to find him bending over her, so close she could feel his breath on her cheek. She noticed that those disturbing eyes of his were as hazel as her own, and wondered that such a trivial thing could command her attention.

"Answer me!"

He shook her again and Diana swallowed and moved her head a little.

"No, I . . . I think I'm all right. But my head . . ."

The stranger lifted her with one strong arm so he could remove her riding cap and push her hair aside with his other hand. She tried to get away from that hand, sure he was going to hurt her, but when his touch came, it was surprisingly gentle.

"No, you have not broken your lovely head, but there will be a bump there tomorrow," he said, staring down at her pale face framed by that cloud of midnight hair. He had recognized her at once as the bridesmaid at the church, and he was a little astounded to see she was even more attractive up close than she had been at a distance. Not pretty, though, he told himself. Not at all pretty. Rather, she was handsome with those wide-set eyes and creamy skin, that trembling mouth set above a firm little chin.

Made uneasy by his scrutiny, Diana decided this had gone on quite long enough, and raising that same chin defiantly, she tried to sit up. The gentleman however not only held her captive, he lowered her again gently to the ground.

"Not yet, beauty, not yet. Rest a bit, for you have had a shock, and if you stand now you might faint. And although I am extremely experienced, I've no patience with ladies who faint or have spells."

His mouth twisted in a grimace as he spoke, and Diana stopped struggling.

"And when do you think it might be prudent for me to do so, m'lord?" she asked in her normal tone of voice, although she could not quite conceal the little spurt of anger she felt. "Surely you understand my position at the moment is most unseemly."

He grinned down at her, lying there on the grassy verge with the skirts of her habit disarranged. "On the contrary, I find your position provocative," he told her. "Most provocative indeed."

Diana paled even more, but wisely she decided not to

show any indignation at his familiarity for somehow she was sure she would lose any verbal sparring match with him. Instead, she said, "It is a very good thing I was not injured, for the accident was all your fault. The very idea of riding at such a pace in a winding lane! You might have come to grief yourself with a farm cart, or killed any child who could have been walking here. Now take your hands off me and let me up at once."

He saw how determined she was, but instead of releasing her, he put both arms around her and lifted her to her feet. For a moment, he held her against his broad chest, then set her gently on her feet.

Diana tried to draw away, but he still held her firmly, while from the distance of only a few inches, he stared down at her. When he was sure she could stand alone, he released her, but he did not move away. Quickly, Diana stepped back to put a little space between them and he grinned again, mocking her precaution.

"But how unkind of you to deny me the closer pleasure of your company, and just when we are getting to know each other, too," he remarked.

" 'I do desire we may be better strangers,' " Diana snapped, her breath coming quickly as he stepped forward.

He stopped, an arrested look in his eyes. "I have it! *As You Like It,* by Will Shakespeare, is it not? Alas, I have no reply for you except to say 'Like a dull actor now, I have forgot my part, and I am out—' "

"Coriolanus!" Diana exclaimed triumphantly. "Did you think to confound me, sir?"

"But how delightful, and how unexpected," he said as he reached out to her. Quickly, Diana recalled herself and moved farther away from him, shaking her head as she did so. "I certainly didn't expect to find such knowledge in such a lovely shape, nor such quick wit behind those sparkling eyes, at least not in the country. Come, tell me your name and your direction. I've a mind to call on you."

"There wouldn't be any sense in my doing so, for my father would most certainly not admit you." At his arrested, questioning look, she added sweetly, "Not a single one of Lord Barrett's guests has ever crossed our threshold. And that reminds me—what are you doing here? We had it on good authority the hunting party was over, else I would never have dared to be abroad."

"Alas," the gentleman said, his eyes twinkling. "Poor Chauncy's reputation proceeds me. I remained behind for a few days of solitude, never dreaming I was keeping the ladies from the fresh air. But if your father will not admit me, what am I to do? I am determined we shall meet again."

Diana shook her head once more. "And I'm determined we shall not. You see, I do not meet with rakes, sir. And you *are* one, aren't you?"

From his suddenly ferocious frown, she knew she had gone too far. Before she realized what he was doing, he took two quick steps and gathered her into his arms.

"No one has ever dared to call me so to my face before," he told her, his disturbing eyes glaring down at her. Diana felt breathless as he went on, "But since you've given me the name, why shouldn't I also have the game?"

Diana started to struggle now while he imprisoned her with one large fist. She wondered why she did not cry out, but only fought silently as he laughed at her. Then he bent and kissed her. It was a long kiss during which he took full possession of her mouth, and Diana, who had never imagined a kiss could be so passionate, felt she might faint indeed, regardless of his opinion of swooning ladies.

After what seemed an age to her, he raised his head and smiled a little when he observed her eyes were dark not only with fear and anger, but with amazement as well.

"I'll not beg your forgiveness, beauty, for you asked for that. Besides, you're too tempting to resist." As his arms tightened again, Diana found her voice at last.

"If you don't release me at once, sir, I'll call for help. Some of my father's farmers are but a short distance away. They will come to my aid, and what they will do to you for daring to touch me, I don't think you'd care to find out."

Her voice was even and cold, but she prayed he could not hear the panic behind it that she was barely able to control. Her father's men were not that close; she was very much alone and at the stranger's mercy, if he but knew it. To her relief, he released her at once and stepped back to bow to her.

"My compliments, ma'am. The grandest *grande dame* could not have done that better. What a duchess you would make!" He paused, one hand going to rub his chin while he thought for a moment. Then he added softly, as if to himself, "Why not? It has to happen sooner or later, and such youth and innocence, such wit and learning, and such a handsome face and manner has much to commend it." He looked at her again and nodded. "Yes, it would not be just if you accepted anyone less than a duke. What do you think?"

Diana had stooped to pick up her riding hat before she went to untie her mare. Now she stopped to stare at him.

"I think if you've not lost all your wits, you're being very silly, m'lord. You're not making any sense at all, and so I'll bid you good-bye."

"Good-*day*, my dear. You can be very sure we'll meet again."

As Diana mounted and turned Belle down the lane, she heard him add in a casual tone, "By the way, you have it wrong, you know. You should address me as 'Your Grace.' I'll forgive you this time, however."

For a moment, Diana's hands checked on the reins and she turned to look over her shoulder at him. He stood there, some little distance away with his hands on his hips before he swept her an elegant bow, one that was quite out of place in a dusty lane. His piercing hazel eyes held her there as firmly as if his hands were on her shoulders.

"Oh, yes, we shall meet again, Duchess! Or should I say, 'duchess-to-be'? Surely you're a witch! How else can I account for this sudden failing of mine unless you've put me under a spell?"

He began to laugh, and Diana kicked her heel hard into Belle's side and fled as if the devil himself was standing there behind her. She did not slow Belle's pace until she was almost home and safe inside the Abbey gates. After she had delivered the mare to a stableboy, she paused in the garden to dust off her habit and smooth her hair. Her heart was still racing. She hoped she could reach her room before her mother or father saw her, for she felt as if everything that had happened to her was writ plain on her face. Besides, she needed time to think. As she climbed the stairs, fortunately undetected, she realized she would need a very long time to ponder what had happened in the lane before she finally understood it. If indeed she ever would, she thought gloomily.

When her bedroom door was safely closed behind her, she knew for the first time how much she missed her sister. There was no one here she could talk to about her adventure—most certainly not her parents, both of whom had shown so clearly what they thought of Lord Barrett's guests. And her father might feel he had to take steps—somehow her mind shied away from that possibility as she washed her face and hands. No, not ever her parents. But how she wished she could run down the hall to Anne's room and pour everything out! Even, she had to admit, to bragging about being the first to meet a real, live rake.

She discarded her habit and left it out so her maid could freshen it. Putting on a morning gown and kid slippers, she sank down in a comfortable armchair before the fire. Her head was throbbing now, but she ignored it.

So, he was a duke, was he? Could a duke also be a rake? She didn't know but she supposed so. But what had he meant about her becoming a duchess? The man *must* be mad. Certainly she knew he was dangerous. And what had he meant when he said she was "tempting," and called her "beauty"? She rose and went to her mirror, half-thinking she must have changed in some miraculous way, and then she sighed. There she was—the same thin face with those ordinary hazel eyes looking much too big as always, and that undistinguished nose and too wide mouth. The man *had* to be mad! Without thinking, she put her fingers up to touch her lips, the same lips he had kissed so passionately only a little while ago. As she stared at her reflection, she knew that even though she had been frightened and angry, at the same time she had wanted him to kiss her; that she had been waiting to find out what it would be like. Worse, even, before he had lifted his head, she had begun to respond and kiss him back. She dropped her hand as if it were a hot poker and squirmed a little under her gown. Perhaps he had not noticed that? Oh, pray he had not noticed!

At that moment, in Lord Barrett's library, lolling before the fire and waiting for his solitary luncheon to be announced, William John St. Denis Rawlings, the Duke of Clare, the Earl of Brecken, and the Lord of Hentings and Stark, lifted his glass of wine in silent tribute to those selfsame lips and smiled lazily to himself. For of course, he most assuredly *had* noticed.

2

Fitton, Lord Barrett's butler, was delighted the duke had decided to remain at the Hall after the hunting party took its leave, for he felt that in serving a duke he had at last achieved his rightful place in the world and the prominence to which he had so long aspired. Accordingly, his step became even more stately and deliberate, his tone of voice loftier, and his expression more forbidding.

Now he poured the duke another glass of wine, bowing reverently as he did so before he frowned at the footman who was so slow to serve the veal marsala.

"Tell me, Fitton, if you please, about the family in the neighborhood who just married off a daughter a few weeks ago," the duke said as he began to cut his veal.

The butler came to stand to one side of the duke's chair. He looked into space as he answered, for he felt it would be rude to watch such an exalted person actually eating.

"That would be the older Travis daughter, Anne by name, Your Grace. She married Viscount Stafford. The Travis's estate adjoins m'lord Barrett's on the northeast, Your Grace. They have lived there forever; a good family, although of course not titled. I have heard it said, however, the family is very wealthy and well connected."

He paused and cleared his throat. "I believe Mrs. Travis is related to Lady Michaels. Her husband claims kinship with Lord Carrington. He is also distantly related to the Duke of Kent."

He paused as if afraid he had said too much, and the duke waved his fork at him, wondering as he did so where servants got their information; they certainly seemed to know everything.

"I take it the Travises do not care for Chauncy, er, Lord Barrett?" he asked casually.

Fitton flushed slightly. "As to that, Your Grace, I am sure I cannot say. There is no visiting back and forth you see, but for what reason I do not know. M'lord is so seldom here—perhaps at one time there was a quarrel—and I have heard Mr. Travis does not *quite* approve—that is . . ."

Clare chuckled. "So I have been told myself. Don't make a to-do, man. We both know what Chauncy is like."

"Just so, Your Grace," Fitton agreed, still staring straight ahead. It was not his place to tell the duke his cousin, Lord Barrett, had been shunned by most of the neighborhood since his youth, and he was extremely glad that was the case.

"Tell me of the rest of the family. There are other daughters; sons, perhaps?"

"There is one other daughter, Your Grace, a Miss Diana Travis. She is two years younger than her sister, Your Grace."

Clare indicated he had finished his veal. As he did so, he wished Fitton would not refer to his ducal state quite so frequently. To avoid hearing any more of it, he finished his meal in thoughtful silence. At last he threw down his napkin and rose, the butler hastening to pull out his chair. As he reached the door, he turned and remarked, "I think

I shall remain here for some time longer, Fitton." Not knowing how this statement gladdened the butler's heart, he went on, "Yes, I find the air here refreshing, the atmosphere restful, and the countryside a delight. Perhaps I shall even make the acquaintance of some of the neighborhood gentry, accept invitations to ride or dine. I may even attend church, unless you feel that might be going too far?"

The butler looked bewildered, and Clare chuckled as he left.

In the following days, he was as good as his word. He called on Squire Beals and spent an afternoon going through the church with the vicar who wished it had a more interesting history. But the duke had not looked bored, and he had even stayed for tea at the manse. The vicar's wife was thrilled by this condescension, and Clare's continued residency was soon common knowledge throughout the area.

Mr. Travis told his family of it one evening at dinner, causing Diana's heart to jump in a most alarming way.

"I am sure I don't know what the man is up to, to be remaining at the Hall all this time," Mr. Travis grumbled, his thin face set in an uncharacteristic frown. "I would be glad if you would curtail your riding about the countryside, Di, since that is the case, however."

"Mrs. Beals told me he was very pleasant and not a bit starched up. Not at all her idea of a rake, either," Mrs. Travis ventured to say, before Diana could speak.

"Of course he was pleasant! Does Doris Beals who is all of five and fifty if she's a day, and weighs at least fourteen stone, expect him to get up to his tricks with *her*? The woman's an idiot!" Mr. Travis said indignantly. Just picturing the duke attempting to seduce the abundant Mrs. Beals caused Diana to choke on her custard tart.

"I understand Sir Thomas Redding has asked him to dine," Mrs. Travis said next, frowning at her daughter who had to swallow some water to stop her coughing. "I wonder if you should call on him, my dear? After all, he *is* a duke, *and* residing right next door."

Mr. Travis put down his fork with a snap. "I shall do no such thing. The idea, Sarah! We want nothing to do with the man, and furthermore, I expect you to refuse any invitations you receive if you discover he is to be one of the party. I never thought the people of Eastham would behave in such a paltry way, embracing a libertine just because he is a duke. They'll be Your-Gracing it all over him and thinking themselves exalted just because they're in the same room."

He shook his head at such folly before he excused himself to finish some work in his library.

After he had left the dining room, Diana looked at her mother and said, "It seems too bad Father is so adamant. We are sure to miss some wonderful parties, and just at the start of the holiday season, too."

Mrs. Travis sighed. "I know. Everyone is already trying to outdo each other. The squire's wife told me she might give a Venetian breakfast in his honor. And what, I ask you, does Doris Beals know about a Venetian breakfast?"

Diana chuckled, but her mind was busy with her own thoughts. Since her encounter with the duke in the lane, she had stayed close to home, although sometimes she had had to take herself severely to task when she found she was guiding Belle in the direction of the Hall. And now, of course, her father had restricted her to the Abbey grounds again. She told herself she was delighted to be able to avoid the man, and the reason she suddenly felt so moody and depressed was because she was going to have to forgo all the delightful parties to be given.

And so, all through the rest of a dreary, rain-lashed November, the duke went here and there, always searching for Miss Diana Travis in the throng of people who were presented to him, and always missing her. Careful questioning of Fitton had told him the family had not left the county, which he had been sure must have been the case. He inquired one evening of a Mrs. Whitton why he never met any of the Travis family of Crompton Abbey at any of the parties he had been invited to, and that good lady, although blushing mightily and getting very tangled in her explanation, managed to convey to him that Mr. and Mrs. Travis were refusing all invitations at present—although she could not say why—no, there had been no recent bereavement—(now why hadn't she thought of that?)—perhaps they were still recovering from the wedding festivities?—she really had no idea . . . The duke kindly changed the subject before his elderly hostess should have a fit.

The very next Sunday found Clare, with two footmen up behind, riding in solitary state to the village church. He was the last to arrive, and he strode down the aisle amid many whispers and rustlings, his beaver and prayer-book in one gloved hand, to take his place in the Barrett pew just as the vicar announced the first hymn. That good man beamed at him, although he wondered if perhaps he should have planned another sermon. He was not at all sure the duke would find his discourse on the prodigal son appropriate.

From her seat in the family pew some way behind and across the aisle, Diana stole a glance at the back of the duke's neck and shivered, although more with apprehension than anticipation. She did not see how her family could avoid him after the service and she was afraid he might mention that they had met. That would seem very strange to her mother and father, since she had never told them of the encounter. It was fortunate the vicar could not know there was one member of his congregation who heard not a word of the sermon, her mind was in such a state.

What would she say if . . . and why had she worn this old bonnet just because it looked like snow? . . . he wouldn't dare, would he? . . . but if he did, would her mother believe her if she claimed to have forgotten their meeting? . . . oh dear!

When the benediction had been pronounced at last, the duke made his leisurely way up the aisle, greeting all his newfound friends. He was well aware Miss Diana Travis was leaving the church with her parents almost in haste. He followed her in no seeming hurry while Diana, almost overcome with impatience, wished the vicar had not chosen this particular time to discuss the state of the church roof with her father. At last they were permitted to move on, and Diana began to feel she had escaped unscathed and was congratulating herself on her deliverance when she heard that harsh, deep voice behind her exclaiming, "Look there! Isn't that a *passer montanus*?"

Not for nothing had Clare been quizzing the populace, and one very interesting fact he had learned was that Mr. Travis was an avid bird-watcher. Now that gentleman spun around to look where the duke was pointing. Shading his eyes, he said, "Where did you see it, sir?"

Clare bowed slightly. "I am afraid I was mistaken after all. The size and wing coloration were so similar, I could have sworn it was a tree sparrow even though I know they are not generally seen in this part of the country. Alas, it was only a common *passer domesticus*."

Mr. Travis looked disappointed and the duke added, "I do not believe we have been introduced, sir. I am Clare; William Rawlings at your service. It is a pleasure to meet someone who shares one of my own avocations."

Diana seethed. Anyone less like a bird-watcher she had never seen, but since the duke did not look her way as he made his bow to her father, she could not let him know by the flashing of her expressive eyes how she despised him for this subterfuge. Mr. Travis, all thoughts of libertines gone from his mind, gave the duke his name and introduced his wife and daughter. Sarah Travis curtsied, and Diana was forced to follow suit.

"Delighted," the duke said to Mrs. Travis. "And are you also interested in birding, ma'am? And your daughter—er, Miss Diana was it—as well?" This last was added carelessly as an afterthought, and Diana found she resented it even though she was grateful he made no mention of their former meeting.

"My husband is the only enthusiast, Your Grace," her mother replied with a slight smile.

"We must get together and compare notes," Mr. Travis said. "Perhaps Your Grace would honor us at dinner some evening this week? Whichever day you care to appoint, sir."

The duke said he was much too kind, in fact he remarked on the kindliness of the entire neighborhood, and said he had seldom spent such a pleasant sojourn anywhere else in England. By the time they all parted at the church gate, it had been arranged that he would come to them the following Thursday evening.

As Mr. Travis turned aside to consult his wife, the duke, looking straight ahead all the while, murmured to Diana, "And that will give me time to study some excellent books I had sent down from London. I told you we would meet again, beauty."

Diana put her chin up and sniffed, but there was no way she could reply, and she was forced to allow the duke to assist her up the steps of the carriage when he put his hand under her arm. All the way home she could feel his strong fingers there; how he had pressed her arm before he released it.

"Well, Edward," her mother remarked, "the man is really very pleasant after all. And interested in birds, too. What a—mm—coincidence, wouldn't you say?"

Diana wondered at her mother's tone. It had been thoughtful, yet wryly amused at the same time. But she told herself that even as perceptive as her mother was, there was no way she could have discovered Clare's true intent.

Mr. Travis agreed the duke had been most agreeable, but he was somewhat uneasy for he was afraid in his enthusiasm he had been much too precipitous in inviting him to the Abbey. There was Diana to consider, after all. He looked across at his younger daughter who was riding opposite, wondering what on earth had occurred to make her frown so. The scowl reassured him, however, for it made him remember she was only seventeen, and surely that was much too young for the duke whose age he placed in the late twenties. Such an innocent, slim miss as Di would certainly not attract an experienced connoisseur like the Duke of Clare who could have his pick of all the London beauties.

Neither Diana nor her father noticed how quiet Mrs. Travis was on the drive home, for they were both lost in their own thoughts. Diana also missed the speculative look her mother gave her as they climbed the front steps of the Abbey together.

Thursday evening duly arrived, and although the week had seemed interminable to Diana, at the same time the day came before she was ready for it. After much thought, she had decided to wear an old gown of ecru muslin, but when Mrs. Travis came in to speak to her before going downstairs, she threw up her hands in horror.

"For heaven's sake, Di!" she exclaimed. "What on earth made you put on that old thing? Especially since the color does not become you. Don't you remember we decided it was not a success when it was delivered, my love? Betty, lay out the yellow silk Miss Diana wore to her sister's wedding, and hurry! Clare will be here at any moment."

Before Diana could protest, her mother was gone and Betty was unhooking the despised ecru muslin.

"I told you, Miss Di, this wouldn't do," the maid muttered as she took it away. "Not for a *dook*, it wouldn't."

Diana bristled. As if she would stoop to wearing her best gown for him. She had to admit however that the yellow silk was vastly more becoming, and that Betty had dressed her hair very well this evening no doubt in honor of the *dook*.

By the time she reached the drawing room, Clare had been announced and was deep in conversation with her parents. He rose to bow to her and lead her to a seat, but he resumed his talk with her father almost immediately. Diana, who had hoped he might betray himself, was astounded at his knowledge. To hear him talk, you would have thought he had made an extensive study of birds for many years. She noticed that whenever he felt out of his depth, he asked her father a leading question, the answer to which he listened with every semblance of fascinated interest. It was most cleverly done, and Diana was forced to applaud his efforts by the time dinner was announced, even though she hoped his studies had taken many a tedious hour.

He rose and offered his arm to Mrs. Travis. "If I may, ma'am?" he asked, smiling down at her. Then he said over his shoulder to her husband, "I fear we have been boring your wife and daughter, sir. Shall we call a halt to our hobby before they decide to rebel?"

Mr. Travis nodded a reluctant agreement as he took Diana into the dining room.

The dinner was excellent, and Clare was quick to compliment his hostess on the baron of beef, the soup *à la reine*, the crab fritters, and all the various removes. He also commented favorably on the wines that accompanied each course, to Mr. Travis's delight, for he prided himself on his cellar.

Diana was more relaxed now, and since they were seated across from each other, she was able to observe the duke freely. In his faultless evening dress, he was certainly turned out very handsomely, she thought, and his white grin and expressive eyes that sparkled with deviltry would surely cause a more impressionable young lady to tumble into love with him, and probably had, time and time again. Diana ate her dinner with composure, glad she had had such a strict upbringing and was not in the least impressionable.

It was not very long, however, before such pleasant thoughts vanished, and she became very, very angry. At almost eighteen, she considered herself an adult, and yet here was the duke, when he bothered to address her at all, treating her as if she had just escaped from the nursery. It was "child" this, and "child" that, almost as if he wondered that she had been allowed to join them. Surely it would be more proper if she were brought down to the drawing room after dinner by her governess, to meet the visitor briefly, and then to be removed before the tea tray made an appearance.

She did not realize the duke had taken her parents' measure quickly, and knew that although they had welcomed him to dine, they would never consider him a desirable suitor for their daughter. Mr. Travis, with his spare frame and sparse gray hair looked the complete Puritan in spite of his learning and knowledge of the world. And his wife, although fashionably coiffed and attired—and he sometimes caught a flicker of amusement in her gray eyes—looked as straitlaced as her husband. Since he had been pursued by matchmaking mamas for years this was a new come-out indeed, and it made him even more determined to succeed in his quest in spite of their disapproval. He thought that by aligning himself with them as an adult he would allay any suspicions they might harbor at this time, sure he would be able to bring them around to admitting his eligibility sooner or later, but 'ware hurry! He noticed Diana was seething at his treatment of her, but that there was nothing she could do about it, and imagined in some amusement he could almost hear her grinding her teeth in frustration.

When the covers of the third course had been removed and they were waiting for the cakes and ices to be served, he looked across the table at her once again, and added another tiny barb.

"Tell me, Miss Diana, how you are faring since your sister's departure? I am sure you must be lonely without her."

This was said in such a kindly, avuncular way, Diana longed to hit him. Before she could reply, he added to her mother, "It surely must be hard to lose a beloved sister and playmate and find yourself alone, at Miss Diana's age."

"I am almost eighteen, Your Grace," Diana snapped. "I gave up 'playmates' years ago."

Mr. Travis frowned at her rudeness, but before he could reprimand her, Clare said, "Such a great age, *almost* eighteen, is it not, sir?"

His voice was amused. It was obvious he was laughing at her. Then he changed the subject and began to discuss the London theater with Mrs. Travis. I'll make him pay for this, Diana told herself, even as she lowered her eyes to her plate to avoid her father's disapproving glance. Yes, he shall most certainly pay!

When the port was served, the ladies went to the drawing room. One of the footmen was making up the fire, and Mrs. Travis waited until he had bowed himself out before she said lightly, "My dear Diana, I see you've taken a dislike to the duke, but I beg you to control your feelings. He is our guest, and you were almost rude to him."

"But I am not a child," Diana retorted, striding up and down the room in her annoyance. "Did you hear him, Mother? Anyone would have thought me no more than two and ten!"

"Come and sit down before you split that gown with such passionate steps," her mother replied. "To answer you, yes, I did notice, and I wondered about it as well. Clare is not so very old himself—perhaps twenty-eight? Twenty-nine?"

"I've no idea how old he is, but I do know he's the rudest man I've ever met," Diana said as she took a seat across from her mother.

"I'm sure he could be, if he tried," Mrs. Travis said as she opened her workbasket. "And yet you must admit he was everything that was pleasant and agreeable to us. Now why should that be?"

She seemed so thoughtful that Diana hurried to take up her own embroidery and ask her mother what she thought of the new design she was working on. Her mother, as she had known for some time, was much more astute than her father. She did not want her pondering the Duke of Clare's sudden desire for friendships in Eastham, and theirs in particular, too closely.

By the time the duke took his leave, a time had been set for him to go on a bird walk early the following Monday with his host, when, Mr. Travis assured him, the chances of seeing several interesting species would be best. Diana hoped the duke was normally a very late sleeper.

He had asked Mrs. Travis if he would have the honor of seeing them at a small dance to be given next week at the squire's. Mrs. Travis would only say it had not been decided as yet.

"I think you would find it amusing, ma'am," he persisted. "Or perhaps you do not allow Miss Diana to attend dances yet? I know she cannot be 'out' of course, but my mother always felt it best to allow my sisters to attend some small parties in the country before they braved London society."

His hostess said she was in complete agreement with the duchess, but she would not commit herself to an affirmative answer concerning this particular party. Her refusal to dance to Clare's piping made Diana feel a great deal better, and she was able to smile slightly when she curtsied in farewell.

Still, it was strange she fell asleep wondering what gown she would wear if her mother decided to attend the dance. Perhaps the white? Or was the peach silk more sophisticated?

But there were not to be any parties, nor any early

morning bird walks either, for Edward Travis took a bad spill from his horse on Saturday, and broke his leg. The doctor assured them he would recover completely, but that of course he must remain quiet for several weeks.

Diana's heart sank at the news. She had been very distressed for her father, for she had been with him when his horse, a new and youngish gelding, refused a fence and tossed him off, and it was she who rode for help and oversaw his transportation back to the Abbey on a hurdle. Since then she had been so busy, so concerned, she had not realized this accident would put paid to any speculation about parties, for she could not go alone, and she knew her mother would never leave her husband for something so frivolous. It also meant they must cancel their visit to Stafford Hall to see Anne at Christmas, and this was the most distressing of all.

She tried to be cheerful, but the curtailment of all their plans put her in a very downcast frame of mind. By contrast, her mother, after she learned her husband would walk again with only a limp, became positively cheerful. One of the first things she did was write to her elder daughter to tell her of the accident, and although she told this to Diana, she did not feel it necessary to reveal everything her letter contained.

All their friends called to inquire for Mr. Travis as soon as the news became known, and the Duke of Clare was among the first to make an appearance, bearing some fruit from Lord Barrett's glasshouse, and a large book of bird plates to amuse the invalid.

Mrs. Travis received him in the morning room, saying that although she knew her husband would be disappointed to miss seeing him, he was sleeping at present under an opiate the doctor had left for the pain. She did not mention Diana who was on an errand in the village, nor did the duke inquire for her.

He stayed for only a few minutes, as was correct, saying he knew how busy she must be at this time. As he rose to take his leave, he remarked how unfortunate it was the accident had occurred in December. Still, he said, he hoped they would be able to have a happy Christmas in spite of it. Mrs. Travis smiled.

"As long as Edward recovers, it will be happy, although not in the least what we planned."

The duke looked at her questioningly, and she explained further, "We had intended to visit our elder daughter Anne in Cuckfield, but of course travel is out of the question for Edward, and I cannot leave him."

Clare nodded and said lightly, "But surely Miss Diana would enjoy a visit to her sister. I am sure someone suitable could be found to accompany her if it would make you feel easier. It has often seemed to me the coach lines are littered with governesses traveling to and fro. One wonders sometimes how the young learn anything when their mentors always appear to be exchanging posts."

Mrs. Travis laughed with him, and said she had not considered that possibility, and the duke took his leave.

She stayed in the morning room for quite a while after his departure, staring out the window at the flurry of snow that had begun to whiten the ground. At last she nodded and smiled to herself before she went upstairs to tell her husband her plan when he awoke; a carefully edited plan, of course, for she was sure Edward had no idea which way the wind was blowing. Men were so blind! And she herself was not completely sure . . . but she would see. As she reached the first landing, she reminded herself to send a note to the dressmaker, to hurry the new gowns that had been ordered for Diana, and to see if her own fur cloak would fit her as well.

The duke called twice the following week, and the second time was so fortunate as to be received by Diana alone, for his visit coincided with the doctor's, and Mrs. Travis had gone up with him to see to her husband.

Diana knew now she was to travel to Stafford Hall alone, except for Betty, the coachman, and a footman, of course. She was to relay the reassuring news of her father's recovery and take with her all the Christmas gifts that had been prepared. Of course she was excited about the visit, but still she had felt a pang of what she told herself must be relief when she first learned of it, for the journey would put her beyond the duke's reach once and for all. Now, as she rose from the writing desk to greet him, that secret gave her the courage to hold out her hand calmly while she asked him to be seated.

"Alone at last!" he exclaimed passionately, holding his arms wide as he advanced toward her. When she was quick to step behind a chair, he chuckled.

"Don't be afraid, beauty, I was only funning. Even such a great *rake* as myself would not attempt any mischief in your own home, especially when your father is tied to his bed."

"But how reassuring, Your Grace, to discover even *you* have some scruples," Diana said as she rang for the butler. "May I offer you a glass of wine? Your attentions to my father are most gratifying to both my mother and myself. Such condescension! Such distinguished courtesy! La, I hope we don't become puffed up with conceit. Ah, there you are, Beldings. Some wine for the duke, if you please."

Clare waited until the butler had bowed himself away

before he took the chair Diana indicated and lounged in it, completely at his ease.

"That's enough of your sass, girl," he said with a grin. "I'm amazed to find I like your parents; certainly I never thought to."

"I can well imagine," Diana said from where she had seated herself across the room. "Respectability, learning, sobriety, courtesy, and proper conduct—all so much at odds with the behavior of your normal set of friends. I wonder you continue to see us; surely it must be difficult to maintain the pose."

The duke didn't appear to be unmanned by her sarcasm. "You know you are safe, don't you, my dear—at least until your butler has brought the wine? But then, best beware. My patience is not inexhaustible."

Diana changed the subject at once. There had been a dangerous glint in Clare's eyes as he spoke, and in spite of her desire to punish him for his behavior at the dinner party, she knew he spoke the truth. Still, she could not help saying in a little girl's voice, "I wonder you do not ask how my nanny is, or whether I enjoyed a jaunt in the pony cart today, sir. Or perhaps you should inquire if I've been a good girl, because if I have, you have brought me a comfit as a treat."

He laughed right out loud. "That rankled, did it, my sweet? I knew it would. But I am sure you have been a good girl, and when I bring you a treat, it won't be sweets."

Diana was delighted to hear Beldings's discreet knock.

After he had been served a glass of wine, Clare asked for her father, and more details about how the accident had happened. Diana told him of the spirited gelding and the refused fence, and how she'd seen her father home.

"Well done, beauty, and another point in your favor," the duke said, nodding.

"Whatever do you mean?" Diana asked, confused.

"Do you remember I told you you were born to be a duchess? Now I discover it is true. How refreshing you did not faint, carry on, or be otherwise incompetent and helpless. I am beginning to think fate has truly smiled on me at last."

Diana rose, causing the duke to rise as well. "Please, sir," she said, throwing out her hands. "There is no possibility you can be serious. No sensible man would choose his wife in such a ramshackle way. Why, we do not even know each other—"

"But we will know each other a great deal better eventually," the duke interrupted. "And not too many generations ago, my dear, brides and grooms were chosen for each other by their parents, and sometimes did not even meet face to face until they stood together in church. How interesting it will be, reviving in part such an old custom."

"But I tell you, I'll never agree! I don't feel we should suit for I cannot believe I could ever love a man like you. We are too different, our standards too foreign . . ."

The duke put his glass down on a small table and came toward her. Diana held her ground, her chin going up in defiance. He was not smiling now, but there was something at the back of those piercing eyes, some little light of amusement that angered her.

"I am telling you the truth. I am not being coy," she said evenly. "We should not suit."

He reached out as if to take her hands and Diana promptly put them behind her back. That was a mistake, for he was quick to put his arms around her and imprison her while he stared down at her for a long, serious moment.

"You may believe what you say now, but I shall prove you a liar, my dear. We *do* suit, and you *will* love me. You'll see," he whispered.

"Let me go," she whispered back.

At that he smiled at her, then bent his head and kissed her lightly on the cheek and where her black hair sprang up in tendrils from her brow before he released her. As he stepped back, one strong finger stroked the skin just above the neck of her high-collared gown very slowly. Diana felt her knees began to quiver.

"In your father's house I am tied to propriety; beware when you meet me again, witch," he told her, his eyes never leaving her face.

For a moment, she almost blurted out that she was leaving Eastham for an indefinite stay with her sister, but caution warned her to hold her tongue just in time.

Clare moved away and she took a deep, steadying breath. "I'll take my leave of you now, my dear. Alone with you, I find it very hard to act the gentleman." He strolled to the door but Diana did not follow to see him out, indeed, she could not move. In the act of opening the door, he turned and said, "I shall not see you for a while. Business calls me back to town; in fact I leave today. But you may rest assured we'll meet again. I promised you that once before, did I not? I'll make good this promise, too. You'll see."

He bowed and left her with her turbulent thoughts. She was glad she could be alone for a while to get control of her expression and her feelings. Quietly, she whispered "good-bye" to the closed door, for she knew she would never see him again, no matter what he said. When he returned from town and found her gone, his interest in her was sure to wane, if indeed he ever bothered to come back. He might very well become enamored of some beauty in London who would easily erase all thoughts of Diana Travis from his mind.

She drew a shaky breath and told herself that of course such a deliverance from his attentions made her very happy. Then she shook her head, impatient that she should bother to lie to herself. It was true that such a great rake as the Duke of Clare could, and probably would, forget her in a moment, but it would be a very long time before she would be able to forget him.

A very long time indeed.

3

When Diana finally climbed into her father's traveling carriage a week later, it was with a sense of relief that at last she would be able to sit down. For some reason, her mother had wanted her to be on her way as soon as possible, probably because Christmas was drawing near and there was always the possibility of delay from winter storms at this time of year. Diana had been very busy with hurried preparations as a consequence. The dressmaker delivered her new gowns, and some parcels containing her new slippers and stoles arrived from London just in time. She and Betty were so occupied packing her trunks and boxes that she did not have time to remember the duke—at least not so very much. For that she had to be grateful.

It was bitterly cold the morning of her departure, and Sarah Travis herself placed her own fur cloak around her daughter after Diana had taken a tearful leave of her father.

"Be a good girl, and enjoy yourself, Di," she said as she hugged her good-bye. "I'm so glad you have this chance to go to Stafford Hall. Be sure I shall convey all your farewells to your friends and to anyone else who asks for you."

As the carriage bowled away down the drive, Diana

wondered why her mother had seemed so amused. Eventually, she told herself she was just imagining things.

She might have been glad to sit down then but by the time the carriage arrived in Cuckfield three long days later, Diana was heartily sick of traveling. Her maid was so excited at the prospect of her first trip away from home that she talked almost continually. There was nothing for Diana to do but listen to her or stare out the window at the cold, unattractive scenery.

They came to Stafford Hall in the early winter dusk, and proceeded slowly up a curving drive to where lights streamed out from the many long windows of the front. Gratefully, Diana climbed a set of shallow stairs, looking about with interest. From what she could make out, Stafford Hall was a very large stone building, and not particularly attractive in the gray evening light. Her footman rang the bell, and the door was opened almost immediately by a stout, elderly butler. Before he could welcome her, he was pushed aside and then her sister was in her arms.

"Oh, Di, where have you been, and how glad I am to see you at last!" Anne exclaimed, drawing her into the hall past the smiling butler. "I've been waiting for you all afternoon!"

" 'Pon my word, she has been worried, Diana, afraid there might be some put-off, or an accident to the carriage. I've never known her to be so impatient."

Diana turned to see her new brother-in-law was there to greet her as well, and she went to kiss him.

"No more impatient than I have been, my dears. It is so good to be here at last." As she spoke, Diana loosened her cloak and hood, and looked around. The main hall was a huge room, impressively furnished and decorated with holly and swags of evergreen in honor of the season.

After instructing the butler to have the baggage brought in, and Diana's servants cared for, Anne and Reggie linked arms with her and led her to the library, Reggie calling for tea as he did so. There was a cheerful blaze in the fireplace, and Diana went toward it at once so she might warm her hands.

"How good that feels! You may not be rid of me till spring, Reggie, I have been so cold these past three days," she said, turning back to them. Then the smile faded from her lips, for rising from a chair somewhat removed from the rest was none other than the Duke of Clare himself.

"*You! You* here?" she demanded.

"You should say 'Your Grace,' Miss Diana. How often must I remind you?" Clare said as he came forward to take her hand and then calmly remove her cloak. Diana looked wildly to her sister, and Anne blushed and waited for her new husband to explain.

"Already know Clare, don't you, Di?" Reggie asked. Unable to speak, she nodded, her gaze flying back to that dark, handsome face with its half concealed smile of triumph at her amazement. "He . . . he stopped to visit this afternoon for he has been in London, and when he heard you were expected today, decided to remain and welcome you."

"I did not think to have the pleasure of resuming our acquaintance so soon. But you will remember I told you we would meet again?" As he spoke, Clare took hold of one of her unresisting hands and held it for a moment before he led her nearer the fire.

"How cold you are," he said, ignoring the fact she had not spoken to him since that first, startled cry of surprise.

"Stafford, perhaps some brandy? I think Miss Travis would be grateful for its restorative powers right now—because of the cold, of course."

Just then, the butler returned with the tea tray, and in the bustle of pouring out and handing around the cups, and the general chatter, Diana was able to compose herself. The duke was right. It had been a shock to see him in her sister's new home. She took a sip of tea and suddenly she was very angry that he had followed her here. She put down her cup with a snap, but before she could speak, he said formally, "And how is your father, Miss Travis? I trust you left him recovering in good spirits?"

"Oh, yes, Di, I am so anxious to hear," her sister added, glancing from the duke to Diana nervously. "Do tell us how he is."

Trying to ignore Clare who had gone to take his original seat Diana once again told the story of the fall and the broken leg.

"I can't tell you how relieved I am he'll be all right," Anne said. "Of course I am disappointed they can't be with us for Christmas, but at least, dear Di, they have sent you, and with you here I'll be more than content. We are going to have a wonderful visit; why, tomorrow I am giving a ball!"

Her voice was so awed at the thought of little Miss Anne Travis who was presiding over a ball as a viscountess that even Diana had to smile while both men laughed.

"I'm sure we're all looking forward to it," the duke said as he rose and explained he must take his leave. "I've delayed too long; my mother will be waiting for her dinner, although I could not go until I was sure of your safe arrival, Miss Travis. I look forward to seeing you at the ball tomorrow night. You must save me a dance. No, no, do not get up"—(although Diana had made no move to do so)—"as old friends we'll not stand on ceremony." Waving carelessly, he left the room, Reggie in his wake.

"Anne, how could you have that man here?" Diana demanded. "How terrible this is, why, he must live right next door."

"Hardly next door. Although our estates are adjacent, he has a ride of several miles to reach Clare Court. It is his main seat and enormous. Clare boasts some nine hundred acres."

She furrowed her brow. "But why are you so upset, Di? The duke told us you were acquainted, for he had met you in Eastham. How I laughed when I discovered he had been one of Lord Barrett's houseguests! You remember we were always dying to meet a real rake, although Reggie says he's really no such thing."

"I'll tell you everything later, Anne," Diana said, ignoring that last sentence. If only her sister knew! "It was just such a surprise to discover him here when I felt I was free of him forever after I left the Abbey."

Anne had a hundred questions but she could see her sister was tired; indeed, she was rubbing her forehead and frowning, and Anne knew that meant Diana was getting a headache. Wisely, she said no more but went to draw her sister to her feet.

"I'm longing to hear all your news, my dear, but let me take you to your rooms now. I've arranged for you to have dinner served there. I was sure, you see, you would be too tired to join us tonight."

Diana smiled her gratitude. How kind Anne was, how dear. If only the duke were not here, what a wonderful time she would have had at Stafford Hall.

When Anne showed her into a suite of rooms, she found Betty already bustling about, unpacking. There was a cheerful blaze in the fireplace of her bedroom, and her nightrobe was already laid across the foot of the bed. The room was beautifully furnished, but she did not comment on it as Anne and Betty discussed the news of Eastham while she undressed and washed.

"I'll have your dinner sent up presently, dear," Anne promised as she came and kissed her. "And I'll be very noble and not say another word until tomorrow when you're feeling more the thing. Get a good rest—how lovely it is to be together again!"

With one last wave, Anne was gone and Diana climbed gratefully into the big four-poster and settled down on the pillows. She ate very little when her tray arrived, and as Betty was taking it away, asked not to be disturbed in the morning till she should ring. The maid nodded, knowing something was bothering Miss Di, although she did not ask what that might be.

When Diana awoke the following morning it was very early, and for a moment as she stared up at the canopy overhead, she could not imagine where she was. Then it all came flooding back—Stafford Hall, Anne and Reggie—and the Duke of Clare right next door, well, only a few miles away. Groaning, she snuggled back down on the pillows again to ponder the problem.

How had he known she was going to be here, rather than at the Abbey? Had her mother told him of the visit? It seemed most unlike her! And certainly Clare had not mentioned his estate was so close, or her mother would never have allowed her to come here alone. How horrified her father would be if he knew of her predicament. And however was she to deal with it?

It was obvious the duke came and went much as he pleased, and here she would not be anywhere near as protected as she had been at home. It would be almost impossible to avoid him. And how truly despicable it had been of him to startle her the way he had last evening. He had enjoyed it, too. She could tell.

She rang for Betty. She would get up, dress, and have breakfast. Perhaps if Anne slept late, she would have time to make plans before she had to tell her everything.

But this was not to be. Anne, overcome by the thought of her first large party, was up as early as her sister. By the time Diana was eating breakfast in her private sitting room, Anne had gone over her lists with her patient housekeeper one more time, and, feeling herself to be very much in the way of the busy servants had come to her sister's rooms.

"I am so glad you are up, Di," she said as she took the seat opposite. "I trust you slept well?"

Without waiting for a reply, she hurried on, "I have just been overseeing the preparations for the ball, not there was any need for it. The dowager Lady Stafford has such good servants. I did not have a chance to tell you how sorry she was to miss you. Unfortunately, she was called away to Uncle Roger—Lord Maitland, I mean—a week ago. Some illness, I believe. But Cornelia remained here. I hope you like Cornelia, Di." From her tone there seemed to be some doubt about this, but she hurried on, "And Harry and Gregory went with her, and Tilden, of course."

"I will try very hard to like *Cornelia*. Who is she? And although I met Lady Stafford and Reggie's younger brothers at the wedding, I have no idea who *Uncle Roger* is, nor *Tilden,*" Diana said, laughing a little at one of her sister's typically confused statements.

"How silly of me, of course you don't! Lord Maitland is Reggie's uncle. Tilden is Lady Stafford's maid. Cornelia is the Lady Cornelia Ponsonby, one of Reggie's cousins. She came here to live when her parents died three years ago. Although she is twenty-six, she has never married. I don't know why. She is so beautiful!" Anne paused for breath, absently rearranging the serving dishes. Then her face brightened and she said, "Such scamps Reggie's younger brothers are, always up to mischief! They have me in whoops most of the time. It has been such a comfort to have the family here, Di. I don't know how I would have gone on without their help. And dear Lady Stafford is so jolly and funny and *comfortable*!"

Diana thought her sister very fortunate in her new relatives for with the exception of the mysterious Cornelia, she could tell she loved them already.

"But now you must tell me all about home, and Mother and Father; all my old Eastham friends," Anne said.

Unspoken, but clearly implied, was her desire to hear about Diana's meeting with the Duke of Clare. Diana smiled and regaled her with all the news and gossip of home, omitting the one person uppermost in both their minds.

She was still talking of Eastham when Anne took her on a tour of the Hall, both of them dodging maids and footmen who were busy preparing for the ball.

"Reggie says it will not be a large affair. If only I were not so nervous, Di," Anne confided. "There will be twenty to dine, then another twenty or so for the dancing. That seems an enormous number to me! I wish Lady Stafford was going to be here to help me remember names."

"But Reggie will be with you, Anne," Diana reminded her.

Her sister's face lit up with a radiance Diana had never seen there before. "Of course! My dearest Reggie—I am a goose! Come, let's find him. It must be almost time for nuncheon."

She hurried her sister back to the main hall where the butler told her the viscount had been held up on estate business but had sent a message asking them to wait for him in the library where he would join them for sherry as soon as possible.

Taking a seat by the fire there, Anne sighed. "I cannot tell you, Di, how happy I am. I can hardly wait for you to fall in love yourself so you can find out how wonderful marriage is. It is so hard to put into words."

Diana laughed at her blushing sister as she sat down across from her. "That won't be for quite a while, Anne. If Father's leg does not heal properly, I can't imagine Mother leaving him to take me to London in the spring. And I may not be as lucky as you were when Reggie, visiting friends in Eastham, fell head over heels in love with you. Besides, I'm in no hurry to marry, truly, I'm *not.*"

Anne smiled at her sister's sudden frown. "You're very vehement, but someday you'll see. Now, tell me all about the duke. Where did you meet him? How? And how did he further the acquaintance when Father feels as he does about Lord Barrett's guests? Why, he told me he had even been to dine at the Abbey, which I could hardly credit."

She paused for breath, and Diana gave her a very condensed version of that first meeting and their meetings thereafter. As she did so, she remembered how she had wished Anne had still been at home so she could run and tell her everything. But now, seated across from her, looking into her clear blue eyes, she found she didn't want to mention how the duke had kissed her, not once but twice. Even so, Anne clapped her hands when she ended, and said, "It is just like a story, so romantic! Wouldn't it be wonderful if you fell in love with each other and married? We would be neighbors for the rest of our lives, seeing each other often, watching our children grow up playing together—how happy we would all be!"

"Don't even think such a thing, Anne!" Diane said quickly. "I would never accept an offer from Clare. Not that he would make one, of course."

Anne was about to ask why she disliked the duke so much until she remembered she had thought him a frightening man herself. And that was strange, for he had been both polite and charming yesterday afternoon. But she had always been aware of the iron will under the handsome, smiling facade he showed the social world. Perhaps he frightened Diana, too? She looked at her sister thoughtfully. Of the pair of them, Diana had always had more courage, indeed, she could not remember her being afraid of anything. But before she could question her further, Reggie came in.

Diana had never been so glad to see anyone, for she had sensed the questions hovering on her sister's lips—questions she would so much rather not answer.

She did not meet the elusive Lady Cornelia Ponsonby until later that day, for the lady had been out visiting friends. The two sisters had just settled down over the teacups in Anne's private sitting room when Lady Cornelia joined them.

"Dear Anne, forgive my tardiness, if you please," she said. "Lady Barclay insisted I remain to meet her tiresome nephew, and I was forced to comply."

As she spoke in a deep, husky voice, Diana studied the lady. She was certainly beautiful! Tall, almost regal, she had a slim waist and nicely rounded hips and bosom, and she was dressed in the height of fashion. From her red-gold curls and perfect features to her fashionable gown of dark brown silk, she was a vision.

"And this of course must be your little sister," she said after she had kissed Anne lightly, finally acknowledging Diana by staring at her with slightly narrowed eyes. She did not bother to smile when Anne introduced them, but only nodded carelessly before she went to the mirror to remove her bonnet and pat her perfectly coiffed hair. When she rejoined them, she took a seat opposite Diana and inspected her slowly from head to toe. Diana thought her very rude, and she was indignant when the lady smiled slightly in derision.

Anne chattered away as she poured Lady Cornelia a cup of tea, removing any awkwardness from the meeting. When her voice died away at last, Lady Cornelia said, "My aunt, the dowager Lady Stafford has appointed me your chaperone in her absence, Diana. But now I've met you, I hardly see the need of one. You are very young, are you not? Hardly out of the schoolroom."

"I am almost eighteen, m'lady," Diana said, the proper respect for one years her elder evident in her voice. Lady Cornelia's brows rose before she tinkled in amusement as she passed a plate of cakes.

"One would never suspect it," she murmured, her brown eyes sliding down Diana's slim figure. "Do have another cream puff. Perhaps two?"

Diana was positive this new acquaintance was never going to be a friend of hers. Their meeting reminded her of two stray cats, each arching its back and spitting at the other. Still, she wondered why the lady had taken her in dislike so quickly.

As soon as Lady Cornelia had finished her tea, she rose.

"I know you and your little sister have much to talk about, Anne," she said. "Besides, I must see my maid about the gown I'm wearing to the ball this evening. I really don't think she is going to be satisfactory, however. She has to be watched and instructed every minute lest she turn me out looking positively provincial!"

Her glance went over Diana's simple muslin gown with its three flounces as she spoke, and there was a tiny smile on her perfect face as she left the room.

Diana clenched her fists but she said nothing until the door was safely closed.

"What a very rude person, Anne!" she exclaimed then, her eyes flashing with temper. "You were right. I don't care for her!

"But why does she dislike me so when she doesn't even know me?"

"Who can say with Cornelia?" Anne replied. "Sometimes she is like that, why, when I first arrived here she frightened me to death! She is so cool, so beautiful, so polished and worldly. Perhaps she *has* had a tiresome day and is out of sorts. I daresay in a little while she will be as charming to you as she has become to me."

Diana thought that most unlikely, but she could see the conversation was upsetting her sister, and remembering she was a guest in the house, she withheld any further comments about Reggie's beauteous cousin.

That evening, as she was being dressed in a new gown of pale green silk cut narrowly in the latest fashion, and trimmed with darker velvet ribbons and matching sandals that she was sure would meet even the Lady Cornelia's standards, Anne came to her room with her new London dresser.

"Now, Betty," she told Diana's maid, "I have brought Burton to do my sister's hair, and you must watch very carefully so you can learn how. What is suitable for Eastham will not do here in Cuckfield, especially in such smart company."

She smiled at her sister and Diana did not protest her high-handedness. Indeed, she was glad to have all the help she could get. Burton assured her in a regal manner she was most pleased to do anything she could to assist Miss, since she could see how much Miss needed her help. She worked miracles in only a few minutes. Where Betty had been trying to curl Diana's hair, she brushed it smooth, sniffing as she did so. Then she drew it up on the back of Diana's head in soft waves, where she fashioned it into a large braid that she coiled into a twist. Anne had brought some white hothouse flowers with her, and these the dresser artfully arranged around the twist. When she held up the mirror, Diana was able to thank her sincerely for her hair had never been so becomingly dressed.

The two sisters went down the winding stairs arm in arm. Anne was wearing a white gown embroidered all over with silver thread, and they made a lovely picture. Viscount Stafford was waiting for them with Lady Cornelia who looked absolutely stunning in a low-cut gown of gold, her red-gold hair caught up with jeweled combs, and more jewels sparkling on her wrists and at her throat. Her brows rose when she saw Diana and she said lightly to Reggie, "But how charming! I detect the fine hand of Anne's maid at work."

Diana's eyes flashed and Anne pinched her arm in warning, but before she could speak, the butler went to admit the first arrivals.

By the time the Duke of Clare's party was announced, Diana felt she had met most of the gentry in Cuckfield. With the duke came a tall yet fragile elderly lady in floating gray draperies who managed, in spite of the richness of her attire, to look positively haggard. She was accompanied by a younger lady clutching a large reticule who was obviously the duke's sister although older by several years.

After greeting the viscount and his bride, the party moved on to where Diana and the Lady Cornelia were standing in uneasy alliance.

"Allow me to present you to my mother, the Dowager Duchess of Clare, Miss Travis. And to my sister, Lady Emily," the duke said as he smiled down at her. "You do remember, Mother, that I told you I met Lady Stafford's sister when I was visiting Chauncy in Eastham?"

The lady sighed and raised a pince-nez as Diana curtsied. "Charmed," she said in a weary voice. Then she turned to her son and added, "William, I positively *must* sit down. These evenings . . . the exertion . . . so tiring. Come, Emily."

She wandered gently away to kiss Lady Cornelia and chat with her with a great deal more animation. She was followed by her daughter who only had time to smile quickly at Diana before she hurried to support her mother's arm. Diana thought Clare's face hardened a little as he took her hand and bowed over it. "You must forgive my mother, Miss Travis," he said. "She has a heart condition, you see."

Diana wondered what that had to do with being rude. The dowager had inspected her very carefully with her dark-circled eyes, and somehow in her one bored syllable had let her know she had been found wanting. Well, that is quite all right with me, she thought. I want nothing to do with any of the Rawlings. She nodded distantly to the duke and turned away to be introduced to the next guest, but not before he leaned closer and whispered, "I know. It is too bad, especially when you are looking so very lovely this evening. Be sure one Rawlings is under your spell, witch."

This remark so unnerved Diana she was delighted to see she was seated nowhere near him at dinner, although from her end of the table she could see Lady Cornelia was enjoying his company very much, leaning close to him to whisper, and causing him to laugh at her sallies. Diana wondered he could converse with so much animation if he was, as he professed, so completely under her spell.

Diana was seated between the two young Follett brothers from London who were visiting an aunt for the holidays, and she was able to forget Clare as first Robert, then Harold, vied for her attention.

It was a long dinner with seven courses and various removes. Diana wondered how anyone could eat more than a small portion of the delicious dishes that were presented, one after the other.

At last, Anne rose to give the signal the ladies should retire. Knowing Anne, Diana was sure her heart had been in her throat, but no one would have guessed it, and she was proud of her.

In the drawing room, the ladies gathered in small groups to chat, and Anne took her around to introduce her again to her special favorites. It was very pleasant, especially since she did not have to go anywhere near the Dowager Duchess, nor Lady Cornelia, for they were both ensconced on the most prominent sofa, deep in a private conversation. Lady Emily hovered behind them, clutching her bag, in case she should be needed.

Soon the other guests joined them as the gentlemen came in from the dining room, and eventually everyone made their way upstairs to the ballroom where an orchestra was beginning to play. It was quite the grandest occasion Diana had ever attended, and so very unlike Crompton Abbey; the richly dressed throng of notables, the spritely music, the flowers and blazing chandeliers—even the footmen standing to attention along the walls in the silver and navy Stafford livery were impressive.

Viscount Stafford came to claim his wife's hand for the first dance, and for a moment, Diana was alone. She could see both Mr. Folletts heading her way, and was wondering which one of them would arrive first when she heard that deep familiar voice behind her say, "I believe this is my dance."

She turned to deny Clare until she caught sight of his mother, both hands held to her heart and an expression of stunned disbelief on her face. Beside her, the beautiful Lady Cornelia glared at her in hauteur. That decided Diana. Obviously both women expected the duke to ask Lady Cornelia to dance first, and since neither of them had been at all kind to her, she smiled at Clare with quite the warmest expression he had ever been permitted to see on her face as she gave him her hand.

In honor of the newlyweds, the first dance was a waltz. Although Diana had never performed it publicly, she found it easy to follow the duke's steps, guided by his strong hands.

"Now why," he mused after a moment, "were you so very gracious and so willing? Can it be you have come to agree with my decision regarding your future?"

Diana leaned back against his arm and looked up into his intent hazel eyes, now twinkling with amusement. Although she was feeling breathless being held so close to him, she gave him a brilliant smile and did not feel a bit mean-spirited to be hoping the dowager and Lady Cornelia were both watching.

"Not at all, Your Grace. Perhaps I am overcome by the festive season?"

"Peace on earth? Goodwill to men? One man in particular? I don't believe it, witch!"

Before Diana could protest, he added, "But we won't quarrel—in honor of the season. I must tell you that now I see you again—hold you close—I am more determined than ever to make good my pursuit of your hand. Come, my dear, say you agree! Why should we waste all this time? 'For at my back I always hear, Time's winged chariot hurrying near' . . ."

"Oh, I think you have a few years left before you must go to that 'fine and private place,' . . ." Diana retorted. "Andrew Marvell was your source, was he not?"

"You constantly amaze me, Diana," he said, drawing her even closer as he smiled down at her. He could feel her straining to put a little space between them, but this he would not allow. Finally Diana realized her puny strength was not enough to force him to release her, and she resigned herself to a very intimate waltz. Still, she had to admit it was pleasant to be singled out by the handsomest man in the room, and when Anne caught her eye and smiled at her knowingly, she smiled back.

When the dance was over, the duke tucked her hand in his arm and led her to where his mother was sitting. Unable to escape, Diana was forced to curtsy to the lady again, saying, "Isn't this a delightful evening? I hope you are enjoying it, Your Grace."

The lady sighed. "Most festive," she agreed in her weary voice. "Cornelia, my love, will you be so good as to give up your seat to Miss . . . Miss?"

"Miss Diana Travis, Mother," the duke amended.

"Of course. We did meet, did we not? My wretched memory. But I am sure we will have a comfortable coze together, Miss . . ."—she sighed again before she added—"take Cornelia away and dance, Clare. I know you have been longing to do so, but you have such exquisite manners. A guest of the house, the younger sister of the viscountess . . . we all understand."

As Diana was forced to take the vacated chair, and Lady Cornelia drew the duke to the dance floor, the dowager smiled and turned her dark-rimmed eyes to her reluctant companion.

"Such a handsome couple, don't you think, Miss . . . Miss? I am sure we will all be pleased when it is finally announced. Such a suitable connection, and Lady Cornelia so worthy of Clare—her birth and fortune, to say nothing of her beauty. She was Earl Ponsonby's daughter, y'know. Dear girl that she is, I shall go happily to my grave when they are wed."

"Mama, never say so," Lady Emily exclaimed in a gruff voice behind them. "Bound to be bad luck! Besides, William never said he—"

"How you do chatter, Emily! You are giving me the headache," her fond mother interrupted, pressing a lavender-scented handkerchief to her temples and sighing deeply. Lady Emily subsided.

"Besides, it is impossible to converse with Miss . . . Miss? . . . when you insist on pushing yourself forward in this unseemly manner."

She turned again to Diana who was watching the dancers with what she hoped was only polite interest. Clare and Lady Cornelia did make a handsome couple, both of them so tall and good-looking. The lady's red-gold curls were brilliant against the black of the duke's evening dress. Since it was not a waltz, he was not holding her anywhere near as closely as he had held Diana, but he seemed to be enjoying himself, bending his head to catch a whispered comment, and laughing before he replied. Diana was glad to look away when the dowager spoke to her again.

"But where did *you* meet Clare? I would not have thought you were even out yet. Surely you are very young. In fact, I am surprised your mother permitted you to come here alone."

She sounded suspicious, almost as if Diana was involved in some dark plot, abetted by her mother, to snare her son.

"My mother was unable to leave my father at this time. He is recovering from a broken leg. But surely I may visit my sister alone? As for my introduction to your son, Your Grace, we met in church."

There was a stifled exclamation from behind the dowager's chair. Diana wished she might turn to see Lady Emily's face, even as she went on, "And then my father asked the duke to dine with us at Crompton Abbey when he discovered Clare was such an ardent bird-watcher."

This information was too much for the duke's sister. She quickly dug into her capacious reticule for one of her mother's large handkerchiefs to stifle a sudden fit of coughing.

"Church? Bird-watching?" the dowager asked, bewildered, although she was frowning as well. "My son? *Clare?*"

Diana was delighted to see Mr. Harold Follett bowing before her and asking for the next dance, and she was able to make good her escape while the dowager scolded her daughter for her sudden attack. She gathered the dowager was the only one allowed to indulge in spells of any kind.

The duke did not ask her to dance again but she was never without a partner, and as she danced, she was able to observe the Rawlings occasionally where they remained seated against the wall. She noticed the dowager was talking earnestly with the duke while Emily hovered behind them. When another couple crossed her line of sight, Diana missed Clare rising from his chair so abruptly, it almost toppled over. The dowager was quick to put her hand to her heart while she swayed alarmingly. The next time Diana looked their way it was to discover with some regret, the party from Clare Court had already left the ball, well before its conclusion.

She could not help but wonder why.

4

The Dowager Duchess of Clare had had a weak heart for as long as anyone could remember. She had married while still very young and, as far as anyone knew, in perfect health in spite of her slender build and ethereal looks. Of course she was delighted to become a duchess, but before very long she had to admit married life could sometimes be very unpleasant, in spite of a handsome husband who showered her with love and adoration. That, alas, was the problem. She did, however, know her duty, and after presenting her husband with three daughters in quick succession, was fortunate enough to be brought to bed of a son after a fourth pregnancy. No one could have been more pleased, not even the duke, for the assured continuation of the line made it possible for her to cease participating in what she had always considered a very unpleasant and undignified activity.

The duke, not a perceptive man, failed to connect his wife's suddenly impaired heart with the birth of their son and heir, and after a few attempts to resume his marital relationship, gave up and allowed his wife the solitude of a separate bedroom. He began to spend most of his time in town, appearing at Clare Court only on special occasions. To be fair to the duchess, she had not fallen into hypochondria deliberately; she had always had a tendency toward a rapid heartbeat when she became excited. It was but a small step from this condition to the constant pandering for what she called in deprecation, "my poor heart."

Doctors had come and gone, and those who agreed with the lady's own diagnosis that she must be very careful of her health indeed, tended to retain her patronage longer than the ones who told her brusquely there was nothing on earth the matter with her that a little exercise and fresh air would not cure.

When her husband died—very suddenly in the bed of his latest mistress—there might easily have been a scandal. The duchess, however, was successful in stifling the rumors that began to circulate, for she presented such a picture of bereaved widowhood in her trailing black gowns and woebegone expression, everyone began to believe the marriage had been so happy that its abrupt ending had devastated her. Of course no one mentioned how ironic it was that of the pair of them, it was the duke in the prime of his life who had succumbed to a heart attack.

When the time came, she married off her two middle daughters extremely well; one to a marquess, and the other to an earl, and she was fond of pointing out to all her friends she considered no sacrifice too much; no, not even the danger to her uncertain health could prevent her from seeing them so well bestowed. Her one failure was her eldest daughter Emily, who after three unsuccessful seasons chose to remain at home. Tall, and all too aware of her plain face and broad, sturdy build, she had resigned herself to becoming her mother's constant companion and nurse. Since this arrangement suited the duchess very well, the only thorn in her side was her son, who after succeeding to the title when he was nineteen, had shown signs of becoming a rake. What was worse, he absolutely refused to consider marriage to any of the girls she so kindly brought to his attention who might cure him of his undesirable masculine propensity for philandering. That he was merely following in his father's footsteps did nothing to endear him or his behavior to his mother.

This past year she had thrown her approval to Cornelia Ponsonby as her successor, and had begun a tireless campaign to bring her dear Clare to the point of proposing to her choice. So far, her son had defied her, which was most unusual, for all her children were used to deferring to her and granting her her every wish. They had learned that to disobey her brought on an attack that drove her to her bed in a darkened room, and caused her to make many weak statements about how, although of course she still adored them, their willfulness was driving her to an early grave. Emily had long since connected the state of her mother's health with whether she was content or being thwarted, but the duke had not yet seen how her spells so often coincided with rebellion from those around her.

Not that she made scenes, raising her voice or quarreling, for she would have considered such displays the height of vulgarity. Instead, her voice would become fainter and more weary in tone, her posture would wilt in disappointment, and her hands begin to tremble. Sometimes, a tear or two would roll down her sunken cheeks. It did not take much of this behavior to make whoever was displeasing her, mend his or her ways.

And yet, on the subject of his marriage, no tears or tremors could sway the duke. He had confided to his sister he could not like Lady Cornelia and had no intention of offering for her no matter what their mother said or did. Emily not only agreed with him, she begged him to stand firm in his decision. Cornelia had more than once ignored her or ridiculed her, considering that with the duchess behind her, she did not need to make up to an old spinster like Lady Emily. Cornelia was just as determined as the duchess to bring the campaign to a successful conclusion, and felt it was only a matter of time before she was wafting down an aisle dressed in satin and lace, to join the duke at the altar. Perhaps in Westminster Abbey? She had not quite decided on the location.

The lady would have been amazed if she could have heard the duke's nickname for her, although Emily understood at once and laughed aloud when her brother called her the Sensuous Ice Maiden. She could tell although Cornelia dressed in a most provocative fashion, and was quick with a melting smile or flirting innuendo, there was little human passion in her makeup. Emily was sure she would revert to her usual frigid manner as soon as she was safely the Duchess of Clare, and could not wish such a fate for her adored brother. His Grace, although not quite the rake his mother and Diana believed him to be, had had enough experience with women to recognize Lady Cornelia's type immediately. Although he was always polite, and even agreeable to a mild flirtation with her on occasion, he refused to come up to scratch. Even so, both Cornelia and the dowager were sure that with their combined efforts, he would come to see the light eventually.

"And, Cornelia, put aside his rakish ways and set up his nursery," the dowager had assured her.

Cornelia had very little interest in nurseries, and meant to cut a swath for herself as one of London's most beautiful and wealthy hostesses as soon as she was wed, unencumbered by pregnancies, babies, and nursery matters, but she was careful to keep this ambition from her future mother-in-law.

At the ball, the duchess had chastised her son in her gentle, loving way for dancing first with that young Miss . . . Miss? when Cornelia was waiting to waltz with him. She had added that she had never thought to see the day her dear Clare would be deliberately rude to a lady she for one was sure was becoming most embarrassed at the position he had placed her in, by making no effort to propose and thus conclude what everyone must consider an overly long courtship.

At this statement, the duke had risen abruptly, and staring down at his frail mother who was twisting her handkerchief and looking sorrowful, had said curtly, "Do me the kindness, Mother, not to be so busy about my affairs. When I marry, it shall be to a lady of my own choosing. That lady will never be Cornelia Ponsonby. I have given her no reason to expect an offer; believe me once and for all, she shall never hear one from me."

At this, the duchess had succumbed to such a severe attack, the Rawlings party had had to leave the ball immediately.

The morning after, she lay in her darkened bedroom, allowing her maid and her daughter to bathe her temples in lavender water and pat her hands while she bemoaned the cruelty and selfishness of her son.

That gentleman planned to go out riding early, determined to avoid his mother and the result of his hasty words. As he was leaving, he passed Emily in the hall. She was carrying a tray of medicines, and he raised his brows in question.

"The usual," she said, in her gruff way. "Do go away, William. There is nothing you can do, and the sight of you is sure to remind Mama of your waywardness. In fact, might help if you were called back to town. You're not being here to remind her might revive her and shorten the spell."

The duke kissed his sister. He loved her very much and he knew her life was not easy, but he had no intention of leaving the Court at this time, not when a certain dark-haired, wide-eyed young lady was in residence only a few miles away. When he told Emily he intended to make himself scarce by riding over the estate to extend Christmas greetings to his many tenants, she smiled and nodded. "And perhaps, William, you might have an opportunity to observe such birds as are wintering over, here at the Court? How delightful for you!"

When the duke stared at her, bewildered, she laughed until her mother's fretful voice recalled her to her duties.

The duchess continued ill for a week. When the duke finally visited her, she asked him almost at once if he had ridden over to Stafford Hall to see Lady Cornelia, quite as if she was determined to forget what he had said at the ball. Clare sighed.

Diana wondered where he was in the days following the ball, until Cornelia mentioned one evening at dinner that she had called at Clare Court and found the dowager duchess prostrate with one of her attacks. Tenderhearted Anne had cried out in sympathy and said they must all leave cards, as well as sending flowers or perhaps a basket of fruit; what did Reggie think? Reggie thought the number of gifts that had made their way to the Court excessive already, but before he could speak, Cornelia offered to take the gift with her the following day.

Just then there was an uproar in the hall, and it was not very long before the doors to the dining room opened and Reggie's younger brothers burst in: sixteen-year-old Harry trying to restrain twelve-year-old Gregory. Behind them, Lady Stafford came in, escorted by a gentleman.

Anne went to hug her, while Diana and Cornelia rose courteously. Lady Stafford waved them back to their seats.

"No, no, my dears, do keep your seats! I could not wait a moment more to see you but we will not stay and join you in all our dirt. Gregory, put that orange down! Anne, my love, I have instructed Smithings to serve us a light repast in an hour. Did the ball go well? I am longing to hear all about it! Harry, take your brother away at once if he cannot behave himself. My dear Diana, how delightful to see you again . . . Cornelia, that gown is prodigious becoming . . . Reggie, dearest son, I have missed you so much, and as you can see, I've brought your cousin Roger back with me."

The lady paused for breath and beamed at them all. Roger Maitland smiled and bowed beside her. He was a man a little older than Reggie, with a pleasant face, a fresh complexion, and very dark hair neatly arranged.

"You know everyone, Roger, do you not? Oh, no, of course you have not met Anne's sister, Diana Travis, for you were not able to attend the wedding, were you?" Lady Stafford amended.

Diana smiled as Anne remarked, "I hope the fact you have joined us, Cousin Roger, means your father has recovered?"

Lady Stafford spoke before her nephew had a chance to reply. "It was just another attack of gout—the times I have warned the man!—but he is still uncomfortable, and even though I should not say this to your face, Roger, your father is the very devil when he is ill. He always was. I have brought Roger here so he at least could have a happy Christmas." She saw Reggie frowning at her and added, "Well, I am only telling the truth. I know my brother."

Mr. Maitland was quick to agree in a pleasant baritone. "Don't apologize, Aunt Harriet. No one knows better than I what a bear my father is when he has the gout. I was delighted to remove from his vicinity."

His eyes went around the table, and he had a special nod and a smile for Diana. She thought him a very attractive man, and she was delighted to see everyone for the Hall had been quiet with only her sister, Reggie, and Cornelia in residence. But she was sure from what Anne had told her that Lady Stafford would stir them all up, to say nothing of the two younger boys who were even now disappearing through the dining room door, each devouring an apple tart while they clutched another in reserve. Obviously they feared starvation before their supper was served.

The drawing room was a lively place that evening, and Diana truly enjoyed the brisk conversations, the jokes, and the laughter as the family caught each other up on their news. She decided there was a lot to be said for large families, especially since Cornelia had excused herself early with a little *moue* of distaste for Gregory's exuberant tales and noisy plans.

"Cousin Diana," he was saying now, "it's been so cold the lake is sure to be frozen. Do you skate? We can try it tomorrow!"

Diana said she did indeed, but she had not thought to bring her skates with her. Lady Stafford interrupted to say, "Never fear, Diana, I shall give you mine since I haven't used them for years. Of course they may be too small. I have a very tiny foot."

She extended one little sandal and smiled down at it with such pride everyone laughed. Lady Stafford was a round dumpling of a woman and her feet were the only tiny things about her.

When Harry also applauded the scheme, Reggie told his brothers there would be no skating until one of the gardeners had tested the ice to make sure it was safe.

"How fortunate there has been no snow," Anne remarked. "Let's get up a party, Reggie. Just a few couples, you know, those who would enjoy the frolic. We can adjourn to the Hall when we get chilled. Both Di and I love to skate."

Reggie agreed at once, happy to please his bride and not at all loathe to forget his dignity and don a pair of skates again. Roger was quick to say he would join the party as well and Lady Stafford looked at them all fondly.

The very next morning, Gregory discovered Diana alone in the breakfast room and begged her to hurry so they might be the first on the ice. Diana knew Anne was writing invitations to the skating party to be held in three days' time, Reggie was busy with his estate manager, and Lady Stafford had not made an appearance as yet although Cornelia had already driven over the Clare Court to call on the ailing dowager duchess.

When she asked him whether the ice had been tested, Gregory was quick to assure her it had, although he felt a twinge of guilt as he said it. His brother had yet to send a man onto the ice, but he told himself stoutly he himself had tested it thoroughly only minutes before, so what he told his new cousin was not *really* a lie.

After dressing warmly and finding Diana a pair of skates, the two made their way to the lake. Diana was looking forward to the exercise and the thrill of being first on that smooth, frozen surface in spite of the cold.

For an hour or so, she and Gregory skated back and forth, laughing at each other when they tried a particularly fancy turn, some of which sent Gregory sprawling. He thought Diana a great gun, and much more fun than her sister who spent so much time blushing and looking at his brother Reggie in such a soppy way. Harry and Roger Maitland spotted the pair of them from the library windows and came out to join them just as Lady Cornelia's carriage came up the drive. Diana noticed she was being escorted by the Duke of Clare, and was glad when Harry grabbed her hand and spun her away down the lake.

The duke, on his way out for a ride had chanced to meet Cornelia coming down the steps to her carriage, and he was forced to stop and converse.

"My dear Clare," she said as he helped her to her seat, "how intrepid of you to ride on such a cold morning. Perhaps I can entice you to come with me to the Hall? Lady Stafford has just returned home and I know she would like to see you."

The duke agreed, pleased to be going to Diana's vicinity. Since Lady Cornelia was delighted to have captured him for her own purposes, it was a contented couple who halted to watch the skaters later.

"How charming to see the children enjoying themselves," Cornelia remarked through the open window of the carriage. "Gregory and Harry have so much energy it is good to see them using it outdoors instead of in their mama's drawing room."

She sounded more than a little tart, and then she added, "And there is little Diana Travis as well. But then, she is hardly more than a child herself." There was a pause before she went on in a curiously flat voice, "And Roger Maitland; how kind of him to keep the children company."

Cornelia stole a glance at the duke. There was a faint smile on his face as he watched the four skaters gliding and twirling so gracefully on the ice. Diana was dressed in a dark red gown and cape with a matching cap and a scarf that floated behind her as she moved. He could hear her gay laughter clearly in the crisp air.

Suddenly he heard an ominous cracking sound as well. Harry had left her to speed back and challenge his brother to a race, and Diana, who had no desire to go anywhere near the duke, had skated away toward a small stream that fed the lake near a point of land. There was no way she could have known the ice was weak here for there was an underground spring that never froze, no matter how cold the weather. In another day or so, the ice would have been strong enough to hold her, but now it broke up so quickly she did not have a chance to escape, and found herself sliding into a black hole that appeared suddenly before her.

The water temperature was frigid and she gasped in shock, even as she tried to pull herself out. She despaired when she realized her efforts were only breaking up the ice even more, and she looked toward the others for help. Roger Maitland, who had heard the cracking sound sooner than the duke, and who had immediately picked up a large fallen branch on the shore of the lake, was speeding to her rescue, and it helped her control her panic, knowing that help was on the way. Now he stretched out prone on the ice some distance away from her and edged closer cautiously, extending the branch with both hands. When he ordered her to grab hold while he pulled her out, Diana was not sure her frozen hands would be of any use. Already she had no feeling in her lower body.

Fortunately, Mr. Maitland was very strong, and it was only a minute before he had her out of the water and was dragging her away from the dangerous area. Diana shivered and shook as she hung on doggedly and tried to ignore the continuous cracking of the ice she was on. How strange it was, she thought. The air on her wet clothes was even colder than the water had been, and she was glad when Roger bent and picked her up to carry her to the nearest spit of land.

The duke had given a muffled exclamation when he saw Diana slide into the lake, and without a word to Cornelia, had raced to her assistance. Now he pulled his horse to a halt, and unbuttoning his coat, said in his strong, harsh voice, "Hand her up to me! The sooner we can get her to the Hall and out of those wet clothes, the better. She'll freeze to death, else."

Roger Maitland hastened to comply, and Diana found herself being transferred from one strong pair of arms to another. Clare held her close to his broad chest under his coat before he wheeled his horse and galloped for the Hall. "Get those two young ones off the ice," he threw back over his shoulder, but the boys were already removing their skates, Gregory looking very frightened as he did so, for he knew he was in for it for disobeying his brother Reggie with such dire results.

Cursing steadily under his breath, the duke halted before the steps of the Hall, and dismounted, still holding Diana in his arms. She was so cold she was shaking all over and could not have stood if her life depended on it. Somehow it was enough to rest in the duke's arms and be taken care of, she thought as he bounded up the steps to hammer on the door.

"Open!" he bellowed, and as if in answer, the butler swung the door wide. The duke elbowed him aside, wasting no time in explanations as he ran for the stairs.

"Have Miss Diana's maid and Lady Stafford sent to her at once. We'll need blankets, hot water, a hot drink, and quickly, now. Bustle about!"

Even as he was talking, he was taking the stairs two at a time.

"Which is your room, Diana?" he asked, frowning down at her. She noticed he was not even breathing hard as she tried to answer. But nothing but croaking sounds emerged past her chattering teeth, and she pointed down the corridor. The duke ran to the door she indicated. Once inside, he sat her down in a chair by the fire in her sitting room and threw another log on the blaze before he pulled off her frozen mittens and knelt to remove her skates, kid boots, and stockings.

"Stand up," he commanded and then did not wait for her to try and obey as he hauled her to her feet and unwound the long red scarf she had been wearing. Her cape and knitted cap followed, but when he began to unbutton her gown, Diana put up one cold hand to stop him.

"N . . . n . . . nn . . . no," she managed to say.

Clare did not stop undoing the tiny buttons that marched down the front of her gown, even as he shook off her hand. "Don't be so silly! You'd take an hour with those frozen hands, and if you don't get out of these wet clothes as soon as possible, you'll be very ill. Don't worry. It's hardly the time for dalliance, even if I were attracted to someone who looks more like a drowned rat with a blue complexion than a lovely girl. Stand still, now!"

Diana knew he was right, but still she was delighted to see Betty rush into the room carrying several towels and a warm nightgown. The duke surrendered his position to the maid, and when he saw she had no intention of undressing her mistress in front of him, he hastened to take his leave. Over his shoulder, he said, "Get her undressed and rub her down well to restore circulation, especially her hands and feet, before you put her to bed. I'll have hot water bottles sent up, and a hot drink . . . ah, there you are, Lady Stafford. Miss Travis fell through the ice, but I think all will be well."

As Betty removed her last wet garment, Diana heard Lady Stafford's startled cry. A moment later, the motherly lady bustled in to help Betty rub her dry before the warm nightgown was dropped over her head. For the next several minutes there was a parade of maids coming and going, making up the fire, bringing tea and hot water bottles, but at last Diana snuggled down under her blankets, and feeling blessedly warm at last, fell into an exhausted sleep.

Down in the drawing room, Clare paced impatiently up and down, muttering to himself about a household that was so careless it allowed its guests to indulge in dangerous activities, and it was here Cornelia found him.

"Why, Clare, there is no need for such impassioned striding, unless you are trying to keep warm, that is. How damp you are," she said, a slight smile on her face. "I must tell you you were superb, sir, the way you dashed to the child's rescue and swooped her up before you on your horse. It reminded me forcibly of Mrs. Edgewood's latest novel." Cornelia gurgled in amusement. "I've ordered you a brandy as a reward for your gallantry. Do sit down and relax. Children never take ill from these little alarums, you know."

The duke forced himself to take the chair she indicated, but as the butler entered and presented him with a snifter of brandy on a silver tray, he wondered cynically if Lady Cornelia would treat the matter so lightly if it had been her own gorgeous self in danger of freezing to death. But then, he reminded himself, Cornelia would never have been so gauche as to fall through the ice in the first place, and even if she did would come to no harm, for the ice water in her veins would more than rival the temperature of the lake. He admitted that was an unworthy thought, but he was finding her constant references to Diana as "the child" unnerving, grating as they did on his ears. He had to smile when he remembered he himself had treated Diana as a child once, but for quite a different reason, and to her considerable, indignant wrath.

When Roger Maitland joined them, he was introduced formally. The duke thought Cornelia seemed a little self-conscious now, even as she continued to chat with them both. He saw that Maitland too was not completely at his ease, and wondered why. Had there been something between the two of them at one time?

He was quick to compliment Maitland on his quick thinking during the rescue, especially his use of the large branch.

"I've seen that done before, Your Grace, so I cannot take credit for it. Once I even saved a favorite hound of mine using the same method. Let us hope Miss Travis comes to no harm. That water was icy!"

Lady Stafford bustled in before Clare could reply, full of her thanks for both their help in saving Diana, as she sank into a wing chair. "Thank heavens you were there," she concluded. "As for Gregory—well! Reggie is giving him a piece of his mind even now, and a great deal more besides, for his part in this adventure. Gregory did not wait for the men to check the ice for safety, and there was no way Diana could know that part of the lake is always the last to freeze."

When Clare inquired for Diana, Lady Stafford told him she was sleeping, and seemed none the worse for her accident.

"There, you see it is as I told you, Clare," Cornelia said impatiently. "Such a to-do over a childish adventure. It is so *boring*. Let us talk of something else. Do you dine with the Barclays tomorrow evening? Everyone from the Hall has been invited."

The duke said he would be delighted to see them there before he rose to take his leave. Cornelia accompanied him to the hall, chatting lightly of Lady Barclay's nephew, new come from London.

As the door to the drawing room closed behind them, Lady Stafford looked anxiously to where Roger Maitland was standing, one hand rubbing his chin and a thoughtful frown on his handsome, high-colored face.

"Oh, my dear, I *know*," she said, waving her pudgy hands in her distress. "It is too bad! But a duke, you understand, so tempting for her. Oh, dear, I fear I have said too much and I would not distress you for the world . . ."

Her voice trailed away as Roger came over to kiss her cheek. "Don't fret, Aunt. When Cornelia refused me last year, I admit I was devastated. I knew she was looking for a better match, that love played no part in her calculations. However, I find the severe disappointment I felt at the time, being refused because I did not have an august title, has been replaced with a feeling I've had a very narrow escape. I do not repine, and the duke is welcome to the lady—with my blessing."

He blew his aunt another kiss as he left the room, and so he did not hear Lady Stafford say absently, "But I'm almost sure he doesn't want her either, and how lowering for her if I am right."

5

Cornelia Ponsonby had indeed refused Roger Maitland when he had asked for her hand the previous spring. She liked him well enough, and it was true he came from a good family and was very wealthy as well, but she had no intention of becoming a mere "Mrs."—in fact she had already refused five other gentlemen who did not meet her standards in the years since her come-out. When she met the duke, she knew she had been right to wait, for there was no comparing him to the others. She did not entertain any warmer feelings for him than she had had for Roger; perhaps it would be fair to say she had less, for she suspected Clare would make a difficult husband, less malleable and easy to lead in the way she wished him to go. Nevertheless she had every intention of bringing him to his knees, for marriage to a wealthy duke more than made up for any coolness of feeling or disparity of interests. She knew she was beautiful, she did not see how Clare could withstand her charms any more than her other suitors or her cousin had. Still, she resolved to be very kind to poor Roger. He was handsome, after all, and so desperately in love with her he had been unable to stay away from her after her refusal. Besides, the more beaux dancing attendance on her, the better. Perhaps it might make the duke propose without any further delay when he saw how sought after she was, for he might worry about Roger Maitland cutting him out. To this end, she stayed very close to her cousin the next evening at the Barclays', smiling and flirting with great animation. She was not aware her tactics were not succeeding, for her former suitor, although scrupulously polite, had changed his mind, and the duke cared not a whit whom she flirted with and was only grateful for the respite.

Diana was not among the party from Stafford Hall, and Clare went at once to ask Anne how she did.

"Poor Di has the most dreadful cold, Your Grace," Anne told him in her pleasant voice. The duke studied her carefully, but there was no concern on her face, so he was reassured that Diana was not seriously ill. He had spent a lot of time worrying about her, considerably surprising himself as he did so. It was most unlike him.

"What a shame! But I think she may count herself fortunate to escape so lightly, don't you?"

"Of course, but *she* doesn't think so. Diana is rarely sick, and when she is, she is not a very docile patient. I hope for all our sakes, her cold is of short duration."

But this was not to be, and Diana missed not only the Barclays' dinner party, but a tea the following afternoon, and her sister's skating party as well.

Anne was with her the morning of the party when a large bouquet of flowers was delivered, and she wondered why Diana crushed the card after she read it, and sat down so quickly, her face pale. Questions only brought an evasive answer, before Diana changed the subject.

After Anne left, she smoothed out the duke's card to read it again, her indignation high. It began formally enough by wishing her a speedy recovery, but then it continued, "It is not that I object to a woman shivering in my arms, but I much prefer it to be with delight. Perhaps next time . . . ?"

What a nerve he had, Diana told herself. Shivering with delight, indeed! She wondered why she bothered to save the card, putting it so carefully at the bottom of her jewelry case, although she told herself it was only to keep it from the eyes of others in the household.

Although she was feeling much better she was not completely well for her nose was still red, her eyes watery, and she continued to sneeze. She knew Lady Stafford had been right to forbid her not only to join the skaters, but even come downstairs. Still, she could not restrain a sigh as she went to the window in her sitting room that overlooked the lake.

There were about two dozen skaters on the ice, and they all appeared to be having a wonderful time. She noticed that the spot where she had fallen in had been blocked off with kegs and ropes so no one else would be in danger on the thin ice. She saw Harry execute a marvelous spin, and wondered if Gregory was also watching from his window, for he had been forbidden to attend the party as part of his punishment. When he had come to her the morning after the accident to beg her pardon, she had forgiven him readily, for his face was so white, the freckles stood out on it in bold relief. His mother grasped his thin shoulder tightly to make sure his apology was fervent enough, although it was obvious he was truly sorry for Diana's mishap. She had told him she was fine and that of course she forgave him, but now she was not so sure. How she wished she were skating, too.

When she heard a knock on the door of her sitting room, she went back to the fire, thinking it might be Gregory come to talk or play cards to pass the time. He must be as bored as I am, she thought as she called, "Come in!"

But the door that opened did not reveal a twelve-year-old boy, but the Duke of Clare. Diana gasped, sneezed, and buried her face in a handkerchief as the duke entered and calmly asked her how she did.

"Why are you here when I am looking like this?" she asked indignantly. "Ka-choo!"

"God bless you," Clare remarked, taking a seat across from her and not a bit deterred by her less than cordial welcome. "I gather from that sneeze you're not quite recovered as yet," he said. "I *am* disappointed."

"Why should *you* be disappointed?" Diana asked rudely. "*You're* not forced to miss the skating party."

"No, but neither am I able to kiss you, dear Di. Not even such ardent devotion as I have for you makes me willing to risk catching your cold."

"Well, that is one good thing about this cold then, for I don't want you to kiss me," she retorted. She saw the duke was about to speak, a dangerous glint in his hazel eyes, and she hurried on, "But what are you doing here in my room? You know you should not be." The duke grinned to himself. He knew very well why she was concerned.

"Perhaps I'm trying to compromise you, since you keep refusing to consider my suit. Have you thought of that? For if we were discovered, you would be forced to marry me to save your good name. What a shame I find you dressed and in your sitting room. It would be much more effective if you were still in bed."

Diana shook her head before she sneezed again, forcing her to blow her nose and wipe her eyes.

"Poor dear," the duke said with a laugh. "But I'm only teasing you, of course. Lady Stafford gave me permission to see you. 'Go and cheer the poor child up, Clare,' she said, her exact words, I assure you. But come, tell me how you do."

Diana took a steadying breath and resolved to be polite if it killed her. "I am better every day, thank you. I must also thank you, sir, as I have thanked Roger, for rescuing me so quickly." She ruined this gracious speech by adding, "However, there was no need for you to undress me!"

As she looked at him darkly, he shook a finger at her. "It was done strictly in the spirit of the Good Samaritan, my dear. There was no time for lovemaking just then. You were so cold and wet, and I meant what I said on my card, you know. I would so much rather have you shivering with delight when I hold you in my arms."

"You go too far, Your Grace," Diana said as she rose to pace the sitting room. Her heart pounded as she added, "You refuse to believe me when I tell you I have no intention of ever spending a minute in your arms, trembling with delight . . . or . . . or anything else."

Clare rose as well and went to ring the bell. "I can see you are on the fret, my dear, but I'll excuse you this time. It must be the result of your cold. Your sister told me you were not a good patient. Come sit down and let me amuse you with tales of London and society."

Diana put up her hands in protest. "Heavens, don't do that! I'm sure your stories aren't fit for a young girl's ears. Ah-choo!"

"You're not so missish. Besides, even though you call me a rake, in reality, I'm no such thing. Ah, there you are . . . er . . . some wine and a biscuit for Miss Travis, and bring me a glass as well."

Betty curtsied and backed away, her eyes wide. What was the world coming to, that *dook* in Miss Di's room?

And what would Mrs. Travis think if she knew? Dear, dear!

"Forgive me for ordering refreshments. I'm not generally so high-handed, but you forgot to do so, beauty."

Diana sneezed again before she asked curiously, "Why do you call me that, sir? I know very well I'm no such thing, why, I've never been pretty."

"I never said you were. Of course you're not 'pretty.' Your sister is the pretty one of the family. But you, Diana, are handsome."

"I am?" she asked naively, greatly pleased in spite of herself with his compliment.

Clare laughed at her. "Of course you are! And unlike all the 'pretty' maids in the world, you'll grow more handsome with every passing year. Your kind of beauty does not fade. I can't tell you how I look forward to seeing it. Of course, in honesty I must admit you are not in your best looks today, not with that red nose. Yet still you attract me. Dear me, I must be in love."

Diana sat down again before the fire, for her knees were trembling. She folded her hands in her lap and looked into the flames. Anything to avoid those intent hazel eyes that began to seem so hypnotizing.

"I could almost begin to think you serious indeed, sir, you have continued the farce so long," she said, hoping he did not notice the tremor in her voice. "But you see . . . I don't wish . . . I mean, how can I know? And besides, it is too soon . . . why, even *you* could not . . . and we are so unlike! You must see what I mean."

"Not entirely since you insist on speaking in riddles. But if I have guessed correctly, I think you are asking for more time. I'll respect your wishes, even though I'm impatient to conclude the affair and marry you. I've been about the world a bit more than you have—is it any wonder that having found you, I should want to claim you? Look at me, Diana! Tell me you will at least *try* to love me."

Diana forced herself to look at him, but what she might have said, or he replied, was lost in another fit of sneezing. When Betty came in with the tray, she relaxed, for surely nothing unseemly could happen when her mistress was so busy blowing her nose, wiping her eyes, and looking so thoroughly miserable.

Cornelia was inclined to agree with her when she came in a few minutes later, although for a moment her eyes narrowed suspiciously at the picture of Clare and Diana seated so comfortably, drinking wine together.

"My dear Clare, how very kind of you to come and see little Diana when she is ill," she began. "But I wonder you dare risk infection when your mother is only just recovering from a heart attack. Was this prudent? Wise?"

Clare put his glass down and as he rose he grinned at Diana. "And how kind of you to concern yourself with me and my family's affairs, m'lady. Of course I'm such a frail little man I expect to be carried off to bed in an hour. Come! I would feel very remiss indeed if I did not make a push to see that the lady I helped rescue was really on the mend."

"So good," Cornelia murmured as she came to take his arm. "Well, we must hope you have taken no harm. And now I am come to escort you to the drawing room, for the others have come in and Lady Stafford wishes you to join them. I've been sent as her deputy, you see." She smiled at him, then lowered her eyes demurely. "I'm sure she thinks when *I* entreat you, you'll be swift to obey the summons."

"Does she? How very unusual of her," the duke replied coolly. Diana felt a surge of triumph over her anger. How dare Cornelia ignore her, talk over her as if she were not even there?

The lady's eyes flew again to the duke's face and her smile faded a little. Then she recovered herself and patted his hand. "Dear Clare," she said. "Always funning, why, I vow you are the most incorrigible man!"

As she spoke she drew him toward the door, but when she would have left without another word, the duke paused. "Take good care of yourself, Miss Travis. I expect to see you belowstairs the next time I call," he said.

"In this instance I shall certainly try to obey you, Your Grace," Diana said sweetly, then ruined her pose by sneezing violently.

"Horrors! Come away immediately, Clare," Cornelia said. Then she added in a cold, disapproving voice, "You really should have refused to see him at all, Diana, but of course you didn't think of that, did you? Children are so very careless and inconsiderate, are they not, sir?"

Diana itched to throw her wineglass at Lady Cornelia, and it was several minutes after they left before she was able to sit down calmly. She told herself it was all too easy to hate Cornelia, for she was the most disagreeable, superior, *unpleasant* woman she had ever met. She even hoped she had passed on her cold to the lady, before she shook her head and laughed at herself.

Diana was well enough to join everyone for dinner the following evening, and in another day, when the temperature moderated, went out for a walk with her sister.

As they strolled along the flagstone paths in the garden, Anne mentioned the duke's visit, and the length of time he had spent in her sister's room. Diana could see how curious she was, and to forestall any confidences told her how Cornelia had joined them and what she had said.

"You told me she would be charming eventually, Anne, but she is no such thing. I'd love to tell her exactly what I think of her, indeed I would. She was very rude to me that afternoon when she came to fetch Clare to the drawing room, and did you notice how she glared at me last evening when Roger came to speak with me for a while? She must always have every male dancing attendance on her; no one else is allowed to interrupt their worshipping at her feet, no matter how innocent the occasion."

Anne sighed and agreed. "But I had hoped the two of you would get on, Di," she said at last. "Since that is not to be, please be careful! I know the cutting things you could say so easily to Cornelia, and think how uncomfortable that would make Lady Stafford, and dear Reggie, too. You must promise me you'll not let your temper get the best of you."

Diana promised, slightly ashamed of herself. When Anne suggested a drive that afternoon to Clare Court to call on the dowager, she was quick to agree to accompany her. She knew Lady Cornelia was having friends call, so there was no chance she might join them. Since they could not get along, the best thing to do was avoid the lady whenever possible.

It was three o'clock when the two sisters were driven away in one of Reggie's smart carriages, well wrapped up in furs and warm lap robes with hot bricks at their feet.

"Of course, the dowager might not be well enough to see us," Anne told Diana. "If that is the case, we'll just leave cards. To tell you the truth, Di, I wouldn't be a bit disappointed if she couldn't, for I find her the most tiresome creature! Then I'm ashamed, for surely it is an affliction to be ill so often. And since I'm so healthy myself, I should have more sympathy."

Diana agreed a little absently, for she was wondering if

the duke would be present, and it was with a great deal of interest that she looked out the window of the carriage as they approached the Court some time later. So this was his home—his principal seat. It was certainly massive and impressive, although she did not care for the stiff yews that lined the drive like sentries, nor the marble statues set about the wintry gardens.

As one of the Stafford footmen assisted her to alight from the carriage, Diana could not help shivering. Clare Court with all its gray stone was so cold and formal and severe. Somehow it was difficult to picture such a vibrant man as the duke actually living here amid such studied grandeur.

The butler who admitted them asked them to wait in a nearby salon until he could discover if the dowager would receive them. Anne drew her sister nearer the fire that burned there on the hearth. Diana thought it was the only cheerful thing in sight as she looked around. The room was dark, crowded with stiff brocade chairs and sofas that looked as if they had never been sat on, and the tables, bric-a-brac, and elaborate draperies, to say nothing of several gloomy oil paintings, exuded cold formality. Diana held out her hands to the blaze and noticed that Anne was almost whispering now, as if she too felt uncomfortable at Clare Court.

When they were finally admitted to the dowager's presence, both girls curtsied. The elderly lady was reclining on a sofa near the fire, well propped up on pillows and covered with a number of shawls. Potions, medicines, cordials, and glasses rested on a table beside her, and her daughter, Lady Emily, hovered in attendance as usual. She smiled warmly at the sisters as her mother extended a limp hand.

"So kind of you to call, Lady Stafford," she said with

a weak sigh. "I am delighted to be able to tell you I am recovering at last, although this is the first day I have been able to leave my bed. And you have brought Miss . . . Miss? with you as well." She sighed more deeply and then waved a frail hand toward some chairs across from the sofa. "Pray be seated," she said.

"Miss Travis, Mother. Miss Diana Travis," Lady Emily reminded her.

"Of course. Didn't I just say so? How you do take me up, Emily! We met at the ball, did we not? But of course that was before my attack." The dowager moaned and covered her eyes with her handkerchief as Anne and Diana took their seats.

It was a very uncomfortable visit. First the dowager professed to adore the little cakes Anne had brought her. So kind, so thoughtful, she said as she waved the basket away. If only chocolate did not upset her delicate stomach in such a stupid way!

Trying to change the subject, Anne remarked how happy she was to see the lady on her feet again. The dowager was not slow to correct her.

"But I am hardly on my feet, dear Lady Stafford. Far from it! Instead I am tied to this sofa. What an affliction it is to have a weak heart. I cannot tell you how it grieves me to be such a burden to my beloved children."

Lady Emily, ignoring this praise, inched her chair closer to Diana's with another smile, and soon the two of them had their heads together and were conversing as if they were old friends. Diana thought the lady very pleasant, and so different from her mother it was hard to believe they were related. Lady Emily asked a number of questions about Diana's home near Eastham; Diana had read the book Lady Emily had laid aside and was able to discuss it with her, and so she had much the better time of it than poor Anne. She, whenever she tried to divert the dowager's attention from the state of her health, was firmly reminded that that was all she was interested in discussing. But perhaps seeing her daughter and Diana having such an animated conversation annoyed her, for now she turned her dark-rimmed eyes on Diana and spoke to her directly.

"Cornelia has been telling me about you, Miss . . . Miss? Do you make a long stay in Cuckfield?" Somehow the tone of her voice implied she considered this a questionable plan, and Diana smiled as warmly as she could.

"I am so glad to see my sister again, Your Grace, I shall probably do so. And Lady Stafford insists I remain for some time."

The dowager stared before she remarked, "I should think your mother would require your services at home, instead of letting you gallivant about the countryside. And didn't I hear your father only recently sustained an accident?"

"That is so, ma'am, but my mother did not need me to help nurse him." Diana did not add that traveling to Stafford Hall at a sedate pace adequately chaperoned could hardly be called "gallivanting."

The dowager pressed her thin hands to her equally thin chest.

"I fear such concern only for their own pleasure is a characteristic of the young. Only dear Cornelia shows a more noble attitude. Why, even my son thinks nothing of the loneliness and discomfort I am forced to endure, and often leaves me to jaunt about to parties and balls and hunts."

She sighed again, much put upon, and Lady Emily said briskly, "Now, Mama, what possible use could he be, hovering over your sickbed? He'd only be very much in the way."

The dowager sagged a little and her voice became even fainter. "Do you think so, Emily? But surely when the devotion of those nearest and dearest is shown, a quicker recovery can be expected. I am sure Miss . . . Miss . . . this young lady's father feels her absence keenly."

Diana was glad when Anne spoke up in her defense. "I am sure my father does miss Diana, yet it was at his urging that she came to visit me."

"How noble, yet how very odd of him," the dowager murmured before she asked Lady Emily to pour her a cordial for she was feeling quite faint.

Anne rose with alacrity. "We must take our leave. I am afraid our visit has tired you, Your Grace."

The dowager drank her cordial and grimaced. "I do not know why I continue to take this. It has a vile taste and I suspect it is not helping my poor heart. Emily, my love, make a note to question the doctor when next he comes about its efficacy. My dear Lady Stafford, I wish I might beg you to remain for a longer coze, but alas, my indifferent health forbids the pleasure. I am sure you understand, as well as Miss . . . Miss?"

"Miss Diana Travis, Mother," a harsh, deep voice said from the door.

The dowager squeaked and pressed her hands to her heart. "How you startled me, Clare! I did not know you had come in. At last," she added, sighing deeply.

Clare strode up to the sofa and bent to kiss his mother's faded cheek before he bowed to Anne and Diana. "I am sorry to arrive just as you were leaving, ladies. Can't I beg you to remain a while longer so I can prove what a good host I am? Just think of all my visits to the Hall."

His hazel eyes twinkled at Diana as she gathered her

skirts and rose from her chair with the intention of leaving the drawing room as soon as it was possible.

"We had better say good-bye, Your Grace," Anne said.

"At least allow me the honor of escorting you to your carriage then," the duke persisted, coming to offer an arm to both sisters.

The duchess looked startled when he bent down and whispered something in Diana's ear as Anne bid Lady Emily good-bye. There was a gleam in his eye and he wore a devilish grin that she could not like for it reminded her forcibly of her late husband. She continued to stare as the three left the room. Clare had not said or done anything outré exactly, and of course it would be impossible for him to be attracted to such a dark, thin girl when the beautiful and accomplished Cornelia was on the scene, but on the other hand . . .

"I think I shall join you and Clare for dinner this evening, Emily," she said thoughtfully as she crumpled her handkerchief in her hands. "Yes, I really think I should make the effort. And perhaps we should plan a small party to keep Clare amused; just a few close friends who would not tire me with endless, noisy conversation."

Lady Emily stared. Her mother had not entertained the neighbors for years.

"You must write a few notes for me, my love," the dowager continued. "Include both Lady Staffords, the viscount as well. And Cornelia, naturally. Perhaps Lady Barkley? General Bates? I shall leave it up to you to make up the numbers. You know my favorites. But do not include that young Miss . . . Miss? I find her neither interesting nor sympathetic."

"Well, I did, Mama," Lady Emily made so bold as to say. "She is a well-informed young lady and her manners seemed perfectly pleasant and well-bred."

"You will allow me to know better in this instance, daughter. I thought her saucy and forward. I suspect she is a liar as well. Church—bird-watching, hmmph! She is certainly no one I care to entertain at a small, intimate gathering."

"Surely you do not mean Diana Travis, Mother," the duke remarked as he reentered the room. "Of course she must be invited if you ask others from Stafford Hall. It would be extremely rude to exclude her, and I won't have it."

The dowager bowed her head. "Of course, if you insist, Clare. After all, this is your home. I know I am but your poor pensioner here."

The duke raised his eyes to heaven. Fortunately his mother did not notice for she was busy wiping away a tear, although his sister shook her head in warning. He ignored her. The dowager had been left very well off indeed and could hardly be considered anyone's pensioner.

"I think instead of a small party such as you suggest, we should give a ball. We have not entertained for a very long time. Perhaps First Night would be appropriate and festive. And if you are not well enough to endure a throng of people, Mother, I am sure no one will remark it or think it at all remiss if you keep to your bed. Everyone in Cuckfield knows you have been ill. I'll give you a list of the guests I wish to invite tomorrow, Emily, and I'll instruct the staff to handle all the other details. Neither of you shall be put to any bother. Now I must beg to be excused. I'm expecting my man of business down from town to consult with me."

The dowager was speechless as he left the room, her mouth falling open in amazement for Clare had never spoken to her in such a way. And to override her wish for a small party by insisting on a large ball was most unlike him. He knew how she detested crowds and noisy frolicking—and she had just been so ill, too! There was something definitely amiss with her son, and she was determined to find out what it could be. Lady Emily hovered over her, sure she was about to have another spell, but to her surprise, the dowager, after one restorative sniff of her salts, seemed to sit up straighter, her eyes dark with thought. Keep to her room indeed! There was small chance of that.

Christmas came and went, and with it several parties Diana enjoyed very much. Both the young Follett brothers had been most devoted, and Roger Maitland was often at her side as well, so she never lacked for a partner. The duke was present at all these entertainments, of course, but he kept his distance and seemed to derive a great deal of amusement at the sight of her beaux.

Diana tried to tell herself she was grateful for the reprieve, but deep inside she knew she missed Clare's attentions and the dangerous, exhilarating thrill of sparring with him whenever they met. Obviously the duke was either giving her more time to make up her mind as he had said he would do, or he had decided to forgo his relentless pursuit of her. Diana could not tell which, but she spent a lot of time pondering the problem. Somehow the Folletts faded into boyish insignificance beside that tall, powerfully built figure, and the duke's piercing hazel eyes that so disturbed her thoughts, or his slashing white grin that always caused her heart to beat a little faster when he favored her with it.

She did enjoy Roger Maitland and always had a warm smile for him. He had a wry yet gentle sense of humor that reminded her of her father's. She was always glad when he lingered beside her to talk, or sought her out in a crowded drawing room after dinner. Roger himself was surprised to discover how much he was attracted to Miss Travis; besides her handsome face and figure, he liked her quick wit and intelligence.

Diana had no idea how closely she was being observed by several interested persons. First and foremost, of course, was the Duke of Clare, who although he could easily disregard both Mr. Folletts, found himself becoming perturbed by the attentions Mr. Maitland paid Diana. Both Lady Staffords also watched dear Di and Clare as well, and were disappointed by his sudden indifference after such a promising beginning. Needless to say, this new attitude of his pleased both his mother, who had taken to appearing in company again, and Lady Cornelia.

That woman had spent a disturbing hour with the dowager duchess the afternoon following Diana's visit to Clare Court, and although she went away thinking the duke's mama unnecessarily concerned, she resolved to bring the duke to heel without further delay, by whatever means were required. That he should be interested in a gauche girl just out of the schoolroom who possessed neither title nor fortune seemed inconceivable to one who had such high regard for these attributes, but it was better to be safe than sorry.

When she saw him nod carelessly to Diana one evening as he strolled across the room to talk to Lord Evans, she was sure she was right. The dear duchess had been overwrought, seeing danger where none existed. Of course Clare was not interested in plain little Diana Travis.

She made her way to his side, already planning a more extensive campaign to bring him to his knees.

Accordingly, she smiled her most seductive smile as she took his arm and let her fingers caress his broadcloth sleeve, making Lord Evans wonder if Clare had any idea what a lucky dog he was.

6

Everyone at Stafford Hall was delighted to receive the duke's invitation to a ball on First Night, none more so than Diana, for now she had the perfect occasion to wear Anne and Reggie's magnificent Christmas gift.

This was a velvet gown of the palest cream trimmed with cream satin ribbons, and there had been a pair of matching sandals in the box as well. The evening of the ball, Anne came to help her dress, pleased at how well the gown fit. It had tiny puffed sleeves, and the bodice was gathered as well, which seemed to Diana to give her more of a shape than she had ever noticed she possessed before. Above the low neckline, her slender white throat and shoulders vied with the creamy color of the gown. The two sisters had decided she should wear her pearls with it, and some roses from the greenhouse in her hair which Anne's own maid would arrange.

When the family gathered in the main hall to await the carriage, Diana was flattered by Roger's admiring glance and his words of praise for her appearance. She did not notice Cornelia's narrowed eyes and condescending sniff. That lady was wearing a narrow gown of dark green silk, so dark it seemed almost black until it caught the candlelight. Diana had thought her neckline very low, but she had to admit it couldn't compare to the deep vee of

Cornelia's gown that almost completely exposed her cleavage. With this gown, the lady wore all her family emeralds, including a beautiful tiara. From the top of her shining red-gold curls to the tips of her satin slippers, Cornelia was certain to be the most beautiful woman at the ball. Diana told herself it was only normal to feel envious, and not a character failing at all.

When the party from the Hall entered Clare Court, Cornelia held herself so regally, and moved so gracefully to have a quiet word with the butler, that Diana thought she appeared the duchess in residence already.

Somehow that thought did not please her, and she was glad to take Roger's arm so he might escort her and the dowager Lady Stafford up the marble stairs to the ballroom. Anne and Reggie preceded them, and Diana thought her sister's blue satin very grand, and Anne, so much in love, in her best looks. Following the butler, Cornelia swept up the stairs before them all, as if ushering them graciously into her home. Diana concentrated on keeping a gay smile pinned on her lips.

When they reached the receiving line, they discovered the dowager standing between her son and daughter. In her gown of floating lilac draperies, she seemed frailer and more haggard than ever in comparison to their tall, robust figures. Cornelia ordered a footman to bring a chair for her at once.

"My dear ma'am," she exclaimed. "Surely it is most courageous of you to brave the exertion of a ball! Do sit down so you might conserve your strength. I am sure your guests will understand."

The duchess sank into the chair, murmuring, "*So* good . . . *so* thoughtful . . . *dear* Cornelia!"

When Diana's name was announced, the duke bowed low over her hand and whispered, "If you continue to tease me with your beauty, Diana, you had better beware the consequences. I'm a man and not endlessly patient."

Diana rose from her curtsy and whispered back, "*So* bad . . . *so* heedless . . . *terrible* Clare!"

The duke broke into hearty laughter, and everyone in the party turned to stare at them. The dowager duchess pursed her lips and nodded knowingly to Cornelia, who flushed a little.

Diana was quick to move along to make her curtsy to the dowager, obscurely wishing the butler had announced her as "Miss . . . Miss?" The duchess gave her a weak smile but she did not seem to want to converse with her at any length, which bothered Diana not a whit. As she greeted Lady Emily she saw the duke's sister still had a twinkle in her eye from the scene she had just witnessed.

As she entered the large ballroom, Diana thought Clare Court appeared at its best dressed *en fête*, for surely the decorations, the multitude of candles, and the beautifully attired guests removed some of its awesome formality. The orchestra was playing softly, waiting for the duke's signal to begin the ball, and the party from Stafford Hall moved about the huge room to exchange greetings with their friends.

After he had seated Lady Stafford beside her dearest friend, Roger asked Diana for the first dance. He had seen Clare enter the ballroom and look around, and he had no intention of letting him steal Miss Travis away. Roger was very much aware which way the wind was blowing from that quarter. The duke, noticing Roger's bow and Diana's smiling nod, mysteriously found himself beside Cornelia, and he accepted the inevitable as he gave the signal for the first set to begin. His mother smiled and nodded, and several elderly ladies sighed over the romantic picture they presented as they opened the ball. Such a handsome couple! So well suited! Diana tried very hard to think only Christian thoughts as she gave Roger Maitland her hand and her very warmest smile.

It was some time later before Clare came over to Diana and detached her from Harold Follett, who thought he had secured the lady for the waltz that was about to begin, even as he bowed and left her.

As the duke put his arm around her waist, Diana remarked, "Heedless, bad Clare, indeed! You must know that poor boy had just asked me to dance."

He grinned down at her. "To the victor, my dear, belongs the spoils. And after all, all he had to do was tell me so."

"As if he would dare," Diana retorted, hoping the loud beating of her heart was not too noticeable to the duke. To distract him, she added, "And I cannot like being thought of as 'spoils.' How uncomplimentary."

The duke smiled at her lazily and she hurried on, "The ball is a great success, sir. Everyone seems to be enjoying themselves so much. How kind of you to entertain us all so royally."

Clare tightened his grasp on her hand. "Yes, yes, and of course I asked you to dance so we might exchange inanities. Cut line, Di! You know that is not what I want from you."

"I don't think I'll ask what you might want of me, sir. Experience brings wisdom. But of course I know I should be thrilled you honor me with your presence—finally."

The duke smiled again. "Are you miffed, my dear? But of course I had to ask some of the older ladies of more exalted rank to dance first. I am their host. It is not like you to be so impatient, but I take it as a most promising sign."

At Diana's quick intake of breath, he went on

smoothly, "But you must know I was longing to be with you, and would make every push to be at your side as soon as possible."

Diana was furious. Ever since the afternoon of the skating party, when Clare had come to her room, he had ignored her, or at best treated her casually. His raillery this evening was mere flirting; he had shown her he did not care. She supposed this was how a rake behaved, all wild promises and compliments that he forgot as soon as he uttered them. She was determined not to be taken in again. He might think her little, naive Diana Travis from the country; she would show him she was as sophisticated as any smart London lady.

And so, although William Rawlings Clare murmured endearments in her ear, and held her close to him while he told her how lovely she looked and how dear she was to him, she did not miss her step or betray in any way how his lovemaking touched her. She answered his most outrageous statements with a disbelieving smile and a shake of her head, and refused to be drawn into rebuttal. She had betrayed herself earlier. She would not make that mistake again. When the waltz was over, she curtsied in relief that she had carried out her plan so well, but the duke, looking bewildered, was at a loss. He was so used to being besieged for his attentions, that this distant young lady who greeted his most ardent statements with cool indifference completely confused him.

He took Lady Cornelia to supper and made himself flirt with her while he admired the opulence displayed by her low-cut gown. His sister Emily, seated on his other side, saw Diana watching, but the girl glanced away before she could smile and shake her head in denial.

Later, Diana was happy to agree to Roger's invitation to stroll about the Court, for that way she would not have to watch Cornelia and the duke. Several other guests were doing the same thing, and Diana found herself caught up in Roger's enthusiasm as they explored all the rooms. When they entered a large salon that contained only a number of marble statues and several hard chairs ranged along the walls in stiff formation, they both gasped.

"I say, living here must be like living in a museum, don't you think?" he asked. "Do you suppose the chairs are set that way so we can sit down and contemplate the duke's art collection in reverent silence?"

Diana stared at a life-sized reproduction of a large lady who appeared to be repulsing two ardent satyrs while in danger of losing her classical draperies. "I cannot like his taste in art," she admitted. "Imagine seeing that every day and feeling you had to admire it!"

Roger smiled at her. "I wish I might show you my house at Littledean. I flatter myself you would like it much better than this formal grandeur, for it is truly a home, complete with warmth and love."

Diana's expression grew wary, and Mr. Maitland, quick to note it, changed the subject as he led her farther into the room. "As long as we're here, we must be sure to see all Clare's treasures. Here, if I'm not mistaken, is Medusa. I've never cared for snakes, have you, Diana?"

They continued around the room until they reached the doorway again, but when Roger would have held it wide for her to pass through, Diana put her hand on his arm to delay him. She had just glimpsed the duke and Cornelia in the hall and had no desire to join them. Cornelia was standing so close to Clare she appeared to be molded to his side, and when Diana saw his slight smile for the lady, her heart sank.

So, she had been right after all, and the duke had only

been playing a game with her. Teasing her into thinking he wanted her, to pass the time, when all the while he was as good as promised to Cornelia. She suddenly remembered even the dowager duchess had said they would be married. What a fool she had been!

"Wait, Roger," she whispered. "I don't want to see Clare or Lady Cornelia just now, if you don't mind."

He drew her back behind the door, shutting it quickly. "Nor do I. We can wait here until we're sure they've gone back to the ballroom."

He smiled at her in conspiracy, and Diana smiled back. How kind he was, she thought. How good and understanding.

But the duke, although he gave no sign of it, had seen them through the partially open door, and he had also seen how quickly they had withdrawn and closed it, and he was furious. How dare Maitland take Diana away from the ball for such a length of time, and how dare he close the door so they could be private? Was he kissing Diana? Caressing her? Somehow Lady Cornelia found herself deposited beside the dowager duchess with only the curtest of bows before he left her, and without the slightest idea why.

The duke strode back to the sculpture gallery, but when he flung the door open, there was no one there. His mouth tightened and he clenched his fists, which caused a footman nearby to straighten his already ramrod back to stiffer attention.

The duke made his way from one salon to another, greeting the guests he met and in no seeming hurry, although he did not linger long with anyone. It was not long before he discovered Diana and Mr. Maitland in his library. Unfortunately, a moment before, Diana had stumbled over a low footstool, and to save her from falling,

Roger had put his arms around her. To the duke, it appeared the two of them were lost in the embrace he had been imagining, and it took all his self-control not to rush forward and tear Diana from the man's arms before he thrashed him soundly.

"I beg your pardon," he said in icy tones as the two sprang apart. "Excuse me for interrupting this tender scene."

He bowed as he spoke, but his eyes were flashing fire and Diana could not help trembling at the sight of his barely leashed fury. Before she could speak, the duke turned to Roger.

"Mr. Maitland, we will excuse you. I desire a few words with Miss Travis. Privately."

Roger looked as if he wanted to argue that, but Diana put her hand on his arm and said, "Thank you for your support, sir. I shall be quite safe with the duke, I assure you."

Clare smiled grimly. "I'm beginning to think you will be indeed, Miss Travis. Certainly safer than you have been these past few minutes."

As Roger made a quick gesture, he added in cold finality, "I believe I did say we would excuse you, Mr. Maitland?"

As he held the door open, Roger looked hard at Diana. "I'll be expecting you shortly, Diana. You promised me a dance after supper, remember?"

"Another dance?" Clare inquired, his voice deceptively soft. "I'll endeavor to see you're not disappointed, sir."

With this Roger had to be content, and there was silence in the library as he bowed and left them. Clare closed the door firmly behind him. The click of the latch seemed to galvanize Diana into action, and she drew a deep breath and started to follow Roger from the room. Clare grasped her arm and pulled her around to face him. He did not hurt her; still she wondered why all her senses seemed trained on the place his fingers touched her skin.

"I shall speak to you," he told her, his face dark with his anger. "Perhaps you were not aware I will not tolerate such behavior, beauty? What is mine, no man dares to touch."

"How ridiculous when I am not yours," Diana said with spirit. "Let me go! Besides, it is not at all what you thought. I stumbled over this stupid footstool, and if Roger had not saved me, I would have fallen. I resent your implication it was anything more than that. I'm not like you—and I resent being treated as if you owned me."

She would have continued to tell him exactly what she thought of him except the duke pulled her closer and put both arms around her, holding her tight against his long, hard body. There was very little of the lover in his embrace.

"I don't believe you, but since you're so fond of lovemaking you shall have as much as you like—from me. As for Mr. Maitland, he'd better not come near you again or I'll not be responsible for my actions."

Held firmly against that hard chest, Diana could only gasp before he put his mouth on hers. It was an angry kiss, bitter and burning, as if he was trying to put his seal on her, and it was so completely unlike his earlier kisses that Diana was stunned as well as revolted. When he raised his head and glared down at her, she glared back.

"You are stronger than I am, Your Grace, and so I am at your mercy," she told him, her voice icy. "But I do ask you to release me. You are supposed to be a gentleman, are you not?"

Clare was so surprised he let her go, and Diana stepped

away from him, never taking her eyes from his. As he watched, she drew her handkerchief from her glove and slowly and thoroughly wiped her lips, and he had the grace to feel a little shame.

There were so many things Diana wanted to say to him, quick, angry words of accusation for his behavior, but when she looked at his forboding, taut face, so cold with anger, the words died on her lips.

He held out his hand to her, imperious as always. "We'll rejoin the others now; such a long absence is sure to be remarked and I have no intention of damaging your reputation, Diana. It would not do for the old tabbys to gossip about my future bride. Come."

Diana ignored his remarks, and his waiting hand as well. For a moment he stared down at her. The anger in his eyes was under control now, but for the first time there was no laughter or warmth there, and she felt a pang of regret. As they stood facing each other, she could hear the distant strains of music from the ballroom. Suddenly a log snapped in the fireplace and the spell was broken.

She turned to the door, and as he followed her, the duke remarked, "I'll have the footstool removed tomorrow since you claim it was the cause of this melodrama. When you are duchess here I can't risk you falling over the furniture and injuring yourself. There may not always be an attentive gentleman on hand to save you."

Diana cringed at the sneer in his voice. Obviously he had not believed her explanation. Still she put up her chin as she was forced to take his arm outside the library, and said in a quiet voice, "I shall never be duchess here, Your Grace. If I had any doubts of the outcome at all, they have been most thoroughly resolved tonight. You frighten me and I do not like you. I also dislike this game you are playing with me and ask you to excuse me from any further participation."

She felt the duke's arm tense, even as he bowed and smiled to two couples strolling through the hall. He did not speak until they were out of earshot.

"But I am not playing a game, Diana, and I have no intention of giving up my pursuit of you. I apologize for frightening you although I did have justification for my anger. And you don't dislike me in your heart. I am very sure of that, as sure as I am you will be Duchess of Clare someday."

They had reached the ballroom, and he released her and bowed. Diana was forced to curtsy, but before she left him, she paused for a last word. "Do you always get what you want, Your Grace? How unfortunate that this time you will be disappointed. A very good, although humbling lesson for you. May I suggest you turn your attentions to Lady Cornelia who appears only too eager to accept them? But of course that is what you intended all along, is it not? After, of course, you made me fall in love with you and the game began to pall. I understand that that is the kind of thing libertines do for amusement."

She whirled and hurried away as the duke put out a deterring hand. Suddenly remembering all the interested eyes of his guests, he smiled and turned aside to chat lightly with the nearest of them, but he was determined to make Diana see the truth as soon as possible. Where had she gotten the idea he was enamored of Cornelia? Was that why she was encouraging Roger Maitland and why she continued to be so cool to him in spite of his most ardent efforts to make her fall in love with him?

Across the room, Diana took a little gilt chair beside her sister and Lady Stafford and tried not to look too self-conscious as she joined their conversation. After agreeing

Mrs. Willoughby should never wear cerise and Lord Dearing was certainly most amusing, and yes, of course, Reggie was by far the best-looking man at the ball, her breathing steadied and she felt a little calmer. There was still a sick feeling of despair when she remembered the angry scene in the library, and the accusations and insults that had been exchanged. But how could he think she had been embracing Roger? And why did he continue to fawn over Cornelia if he really wanted her, as he claimed?

Her head began to ache and she wished they might all go home. But of course they could not do that until the ball was over. When Roger came to claim his dance, she was relieved he made no mention of their meeting with Clare, although she could see the questions in his eyes. She was also very aware of the duke, standing beside his mother's chair, and staring at her as she danced. It made it difficult for her to mind her steps. And then there were Harold and Robert Follett and several other gentlemen to dance with, and some elderly ladies Lady Stafford insisted she meet. The evening seemed endless to her, and her head was aching in earnest when at last their carriage was summoned and she was able to leave the Court. She pretended to fall asleep on the way home so she would not have to converse, and while she was being undressed, she told Betty that if anyone should call in the morning, most especially the Duke of Clare, she was to tell him Miss Travis was not receiving. And then she climbed into her four-poster and tossed and turned until dawn.

William Rawlings did not find it easy to sleep, either. After the last guests had departed, and he had bid his mother and Emily good-night, he went back to the library and sat before the dying fire, his feet up on the same footstool Diana claimed she had tripped over. It was a very long time before he nodded to himself and went up to bed, determined to call at Stafford Hall the following day to straighten out the tangle and make Diana see reason.

It would have been most unusual for Cornelia not to have noticed the reappearance of the duke and Diana in the ballroom after such a long absence, and the moment she saw them together, her lips tightened in annoyance. So, Clare had been with little Miss Travis all this time, had he? She saw Diana speaking rapidly to him, her head held high and not a smile to be seen on her face, and she noticed how the duke put out a hand to detain her when she turned away from him. Perhaps the dowager had not been mistaken after all? She laughed at the story Lord Evans was telling her in such boring detail, even as her mind was busy with this new development. The duke had been most attentive to her this evening, indulging her in a light flirtation, his eyes admiring, but he hadn't proposed, although she had given him every opportunity to do so. Cornelia could hardly believe it, and on the drive back to Stafford Hall while Diana pretended to sleep across from her and the others chatted of the evening, she stared at her rival with hatred. No little provincial miss was going to ruin her plans, she told herself. She would call on the dowager tomorrow to see if she had learned anything more from her son. And then we would see . . . She had always had everything she wanted, and she would get what she wanted this time, too. Not that she wanted *him*, or any man, she told herself, but she would settle for nothing less than being a duchess. Clare *would* propose.

By the time Diana came downstairs the next morning, it was very late. The butler told her no one had called as yet, and suddenly afraid the duke might even now be setting out from Clare Court, she ordered her horse brought up from the stables. As she was changing into her habit, a light tap came at the door, and Betty went to admit Cornelia. Dressed for calling in her dark brown silk, she came in, dismissing the maid with a wave of her hand.

Diana's chin rose at this, but she concentrated on buttoning her kid gloves instead of reprimanding the lady as she longed to do.

"Why, Diana, I am surprised you have the energy to ride after last evening's activity," Cornelia began in her cool voice as she took a seat by the fire. "How wonderful to be so young and active! Now I, although of course I am expected at the Court, had all I could do to rise and dress this morning. And did you enjoy the ball? Clare was telling me all about your conversation . . ."

She paused and tittered a little, and noticing how Diana started and put one hand to her mouth in shock, continued smoothly. "So foolish, my dear, to let him see you privately. I hope you did not believe a word he said."

This was a shot in the dark but she was delighted to see she had hit the mark for Diana's face paled and she was clenching her hands to keep them from trembling. Inwardly, Cornelia exulted.

"You may be sure I do not take the duke seriously, Cornelia," Diana snapped. "I am not so green as all that! I know it is only a game he plays."

She stopped and turned to the glass to adjust her riding hat, unable to face Cornelia's superior, amused expression.

"I'm delighted you are so wise. I came expressly this morning to warn you. Many girls have lost their hearts and succumbed to William's charms. I would be sorry to see you had joined their number. No, the duke's future is settled, as we are both aware."

She smiled again, a satisfied little smile of triumph as Diana reached somewhat blindly for her crop. "Gentlemen of the haut ton must have their little intrigues and amusements, as I understand completely. For now I overlook the duke's peccadilloes. It will be different later on."

She rose. "But I must not detain you. It won't do to keep your mount standing in such weather. Have a good ride, Diana, and trust me to try to bring the duke to more decorum where you are concerned. It really is too bad of him to tease you so."

Together they went down the stairs, Cornelia chatting lightly of the ball, the weather, and which of the Follett brothers Diana must prefer. Diana tried to answer her in kind. She was glad to see her mare was waiting for her, and she was quick to dismiss the groom. She could feel her eyes filling with tears and she wanted to be away and alone before they were noticed.

As Diana settled herself in the saddle, she saw Cornelia being helped into the carriage for her visit to the Court, but she pretended she did not notice the lady's friendly wave of good-bye. As she trotted the mare down the drive, Diana wondered why she felt so miserable, when, after all, it was just as she had suspected all along. The duke had only been toying with her for who knew what reason. Amusement? Callousness? Conceit?

No matter. The Lady Cornelia Ponsonby would be the Duchess of Clare after all.

Kicking her mount to a canter, Diana blinked away her tears. No doubt they would be very happy together, she told herself. They were so well-suited.

7

Diana stayed away as long as she dared, but she might just as well have remained at the Hall, for the duke did not make an appearance. He was summoned by his mother to help entertain Lady Cornelia, and it was from this lady he learned Diana was not at home, having gone out for an extended ride. He longed to ask if Roger Maitland had accompanied her, but something about Cornelia's expression deterred him. Instead, when the lady finally took her leave, he retired again to his library, completely frustrated. He was idly sorting through his post when his sister knocked and came in to take a seat by the fire.

"Very worried, William," she began, sitting bolt upright and frowning at him. The duke raised a curious brow and she continued, "Mama is up to somethin'—don't know what—and that Cornelia Ponsonby is in it with her. When she arrived this morning, Mama sent me away so they might be private, and it was at least an hour before she called me back to give her her tonic. Know what it is?"

Clare shook his head. "It is certainly no secret after last night that Cornelia has decided to employ the heavy guns, Em. I can only assume she and Mother were drawing up the battle lines and planning where I shall fall, at long last, into their matrimonial trap. Ha!"

Lady Emily rose to pace the library with her mannish stride. "May say 'Ha!' all you like, William, but I don't trust that woman."

"Nor our dear parent, either," the duke murmured, his eyes alight with laughter. "Shall I admit to cowardice and decamp, Em? But I cannot leave the Court right now . . ."

As his voice died away, his sister nodded. "Understand completely. But even though you say you are determined not to pop the question, there are ways, you know, for Lady C. to snare you. Have a care."

Solemnly the duke agreed to do so as he poured two glasses of wine. As she sipped hers, Lady Emily thought hard, and finally said, "William, Miss Travis looked very lovely last night, agreed?"

"Very beautiful."

"Do you like her?" she asked next, her eyes intent. "I think her a very intelligent, pleasant gel. Can't understand why Mama has taken her in such dislike."

"*My* liking more than makes up for any of our mother's antipathy—her rudeness as well. What is more to the point, Em, is that Miss Travis will be the next Duchess of Clare," he said, his voice a little grim.

His sister came at once and kissed him. "So glad! Cannot tell you, m'dear, how that pleases me! But . . . but if that is the case, why did you flirt so with Lady C. last night? So many distinguished attentions, the first dance, takin' her in to supper, whisperin' to her and laughin'. Must tell you, Miss Travis noticed. Didn't like it either. Are you deliberately tryin' to be difficult, Clare?"

The duke poured himself more wine then sat and stared into the flames, absently twirling his glass before he answered.

"It is hard not to flirt with Cornelia when she is so determined I do so. And how rude of me it would be to disappoint her. But Diana is very young still. She does not understand that flirting with a woman of the world who knows all the rules is different from the way I would treat my future bride. And she does not trust me, Em. She thinks me a premier rake—dangerous. Besides, I've promised not to rush her, to give her more time to consider . . ."

His voice died away as he thought of telling his sister about the scene in the library.

"So, knows how you feel, does she? And didn't accept you right away? Good for her!"

As her brother grinned at her, she added, "Yes, I know, I know! You've always had such deadly success with women. How refreshin' that the one you want, finally, will not fall into your hand like a ripe plum."

She crowed with laughter until the duke was forced to agree it served him right.

"But, William, am sure she doesn't understand your behavior with Lady C. Maybe she thinks you've changed your mind."

"Couldn't have," the duke replied, inadvertently echoing his sister's abbreviated speech. "I tell her every time I see her, I want her for my duchess. What could be more plain than that? And yet, Em, there was something last evening . . ."

It was not very long before Lady Emily had the whole story, and was shaking her head and sighing over her brother's folly. "For someone so experienced, who has been on the town forever, you have behaved very ill, sir!" she scolded after he had concluded his tale. "Cannot believe Miss Travis is capable of tellin' you a lie. Of course she must have tripped over the stool. Look in her eyes, man! They are so clear and honest. And then to have you rip up at her—pure folly!"

She shook her head again, and the duke, his color a little high, humbly asked what he should do now.

"Write her or send flowers . . . no, not that! Mama would be sure to find out." She shuddered a little. "Much as I like your choice, don't look forward to the spell Mama will have when she finds out."

Recalling her initial thought, she continued, "Call on her, insist on seeing her alone, humbly beg her pardon . . . good heaven, William, you know how to make love! But do not go stridin' about actin' the duke, demandin' this and that, orderin' her about, compellin' her acceptance—"

"Of course I won't," the duke snapped, suddenly angry. "Don't you think I know better than that, Em?"

Lady Emily laughed as she went to the door. "Haven't done so well so far, have you, my fine boy?"

With a final laugh for his discomfort, she left the library. The duke paced up and down and was only recalled to his surroundings when his butler brought in an express that had just arrived from London. He ripped it open and swore.

"You spoke, Your Grace?" the butler asked in his lofty way from where he was placing the wineglasses on his tray.

"Send my man to me, Hibbert, and ask Mr. Canfield to be so good as to come to the library immediately. I have been called back to town. Lord Barrett is in the suds again."

"Very good, sir," the butler replied. He was not surprised for he had been acquainted with Lord Barrett's escapades for years. He went away to fetch the duke's valet and secretary and give them the bad news.

By evening, everything had been arranged for Clare's early departure on the morrow, and after dinner, he shut himself up in the library to write a letter to Diana. It took him a long time, but when he was through, he was satisfied it told her what was in his heart. He wrote that he loved her, so much it had caused him to behave badly at the ball, and he begged her to pardon him for that. Then he asked her to think kindly of him and write to him at his town house, and he promised himself the honor of calling on her as soon as he possibly could on his return, for he was missing her already.

There, he thought, sealing it with his signet ring and giving it to Hibbert to have delivered in the morning, that should do it! And it was strange. What had begun as a delightful adventure toward a marriage of convenience, had turned out to be completely different. It was as if putting those words of love on paper had made them come alive, full of meaning and devotion. He had not said he thought the sun revolved around her, nor offered to bring her the moon if she should express a desire for it, for he would have scorned such easy sentimentality. But he hoped that the very real love he felt for her would show through his words, and make her think fondly of him in his absence.

He was well along the post road to London the next day when one of his grooms delivered the letter to Stafford Hall. Lady Stafford's butler placed it on a tray and would have taken it up to Miss Travis immediately, except he was interrupted by Gregory, who came racing into the hall, dripping blood and howling loudly. He had been out with his brother hunting rabbits with the new gun Reggie had given him for Christmas, and there had been an accident. Harry, who had told Gregory most sternly to keep behind him (although with Gregory's record he should have known the boy would not obey), had fired at a movement in the bushes ahead of him and hit his younger brother in the arm. Fortunately it was only a flesh wound, but by the time the alarms had died down, the doctor had come and gone, and the hall had been cleaned up, the butler had completely forgotten the duke's letter.

But Cornelia saw it on her way out to visit friends, and she scooped it up and hid it in her reticule. She had, of course, recognized the duke's bold, black handwriting immediately. It seemed a very long nuncheon, and Lady Barclay more prosy than she had ever been before, but Cornelia did not open the letter until she was safely back in her bedroom, after giving instructions she was on no account to be disturbed.

If she felt a pang when she read those tender words of love, it was short-lived. Of course it was too bad Clare did not feel that way about her, but that was of little concern to her. In her mind, marriage had very little to do with love; what it had to do with was position, wealth, one of the best titles in England, and several beautiful estates. She would marry the duke without love on either side without a qualm. Perhaps it was even better so, she thought as she frowned down at the letter she had crushed in her hand, for after she had presented the duke with an heir, as surely he would insist upon, they would be free to go their separate ways. She would make him a stunning duchess, the envy of his friends, and she was so much more worthy of the title than Diana Travis. It was only a matter of forcing his hand. In spite of this clear thinking and cold acceptance of the situation, she sent word to her aunt that she was feeling a little pulled and would not join the family for dinner. Then she burned Diana's love letter in the fireplace with a great deal of satisfaction, and she did not take her eyes from it until it was nothing but scattered ashes.

It was at dinner that Diana learned the duke had been called back to town. She avoided Roger's eye as Reggie told them all he knew of the situation. Diana told herself stoutly she was glad to be rid of the man, for in leaving her without a word, he had proved the truth of Cornelia's revelation this morning.

The days passed more slowly as January turned to February, for now there were no holiday festivities. Gregory's arm healed, Diana had her eighteenth birthday, Roger Maitland was summoned home by his now recovered father, and Anne confided to her sister that she was not positive, but she truly had reason to suspect she was with child. Diana hugged her, but she was glad when a letter arrived from her mother a few days later asking her to return to Crompton Abbey without delay. Anne seemed to talk of nothing but the sheer delight of holding a miniature Reggie in her arms by next September.

Mrs. Travis wrote to say that although Diana's father was doing well, she could not like the pain he was still suffering, and had decided to take him to a specialist in London. She had made arrangements for them all to stay with Lady Michaels, and said she would appreciate Diana's help in getting her father to town.

"And, of course, dear Di, as long as we are there, you might just as well remain for the season. Aunt Emma insisted on it, although I do not understand her at all. She wrote something about not wanting to miss the fireworks. Fireworks? In February? Do you think she is getting senile?"

Mrs. Travis concluded her letter by sending her love to Anne and the Warrens, and saying she would look for Diana within the week.

Diana was busy with her packing, and she was glad of the work for it took her mind from a problem. Roger had asked her to go for a walk with him the day before he left, and when he stopped suddenly and turned to take her hands in his, she had known what he was about to say. She wished there had been some way to stop him. She liked Roger very much, but she did not love him. After she had told him so as gently as she could, adding that her affection for him was as for a brother, not a husband, he had tried to smile as he patted her hand.

"Very well, dear Di. I understand. But don't think I won't continue to press my suit when we meet in London this spring. Perhaps I was too precipitous. Perhaps you need more time."

Diana, a lump in her throat, remembered that the duke had also promised to give her more time, and she nodded miserably. He had certainly done that. Not a letter, not a word. It was as if he had walked away without a backward glance, and it reinforced her conviction it had only been a game. And to discuss her with Cornelia, reveal their conversations, perhaps even laugh at her naïveté was unbearable for her to contemplate. Cornelia had let drop to Diana that she had had letters from Clare, of course, but since Diana had no way of knowing she was lying, this only made her feel worse.

I'll be glad to get home, she thought fiercely. I hope I never see him again. Deceiver! Libertine! Father was right. His type is no good at all, and decent women should shun him.

If only she could have seen Lady Emily, she might have felt happier, but shortly after the duke had gone to town, and not with any malice aforethought, his mother had come down with an infectious fever, and there were no more visits to Clare Court.

Diana was only at Crompton Abbey for a few days before she was once again traveling to the metropolis. She had been there as a child, to see the museums, attend a concert, and visit her relatives, but this time would be different, or so her Great-Aunt Emma told her the first evening they met at dinner. They were alone except for Lady Michaels's companion, for Mr. Travis had been sadly buffeted by the coach travel, and his wife was having her dinner on a tray by his bedside.

"Your first season, *and* I wager, your last," the old lady said, pointing her fork at Diana. "How was your stay at Stafford Hall? Gay? Festive?"

Diana nodded absently as she accepted a serving of chicken in a mushroom sauce from the elderly footman. "And how many proposals did you receive while you were there, gel?" her great-aunt continued.

"Two," Diana said without thinking, for private family matters were never discussed before the servants in her home. She gasped when she realized what she had said, but Lady Michaels only chortled and wiped her eyes.

"Pay him no mind, Di, deaf as a post. Not that it matters in the slightest, for servants always know everything, and why not? 'Tis the only amusement they get, keeping an eye on their betters. Polly, take a drink of water if you cannot stop coughing!"

Her companion obeyed, her eyes begging Diana to forgive Lady Michaels's eccentricity as that lady continued, "Two, eh? Most promising! I suppose you won't tell me who they are. That's all right. I'll find out for myself. I knew I did the wise thing inviting you here for the season, for fireworks there are sure to be, and I love fireworks."

"Why do you say that, ma'am?" Diana asked, remembering her mother's letter, and glad to turn the conversation away from her personal life.

"Told Polly at your sister's wedding. Now there's a gel all milk and mild, but you, Diana, are a different kettle of fish. I remember your temper! There'll be no meek 'yes, milord—of course, milord—whatever you say, milord,' with you. Where you are, and eligible gentlemen, there are bound to be Roman candles going off. I wouldn't miss 'em for the world!"

She cackled again and Diana tried to look agreeable to this analysis of her character.

"We'll have to see about parties and teas; getting you out and about and visible," Lady Michaels went on, waving away the rabbit pie but tapping her wineglass for a refill. Diana thought her table manners atrocious, and she sympathized with poor Polly who was even now being ordered to attend her mistress after dinner so she might make up what she called a "campaign plan." Diana began to feel manipulated, and she hoped her mother would take a hand soon and put a stop to the elderly lady's calm assumption that she and she alone was responsible for the success of Diana's season.

"Of course London is thin of company as yet," Lady Michaels said as she led the way to the drawing room later. "Things won't start humming until May, but that is all to the good. It will give you a chance to get used to going about. It might even give you an edge on the other fillies."

She patted Diana's hand before she took her customary seat by the fire. "Don't worry, Di," she said breezily. "Your old Aunt Emma knows what's what, and with me to help you, you'll be racing down the homestretch in first place before you know it!"

Diana burst out laughing, although she wondered if it

would be more appropriate for her to neigh instead. When she told her mother about it the next morning, Mrs. Travis shook her head.

"Aunt Emma shall be restrained, Diana, for I shall see to it. Comparing you to a racehorse—well!" She looked deeply into her daughter's eyes and added, "You are not to feel pressed, my dear. My fondest hope is for you to make a happy marriage—as happy as mine has been—but if you do not meet a gentleman that you feel you can care for that way, there is to be no thought of second best. You shall come home to Crompton Abbey, no matter what Aunt Emma says."

She did indeed speak to her aunt, and Lady Michaels subsided, although every so often she could be heard to mutter that people who thought a knight in shining armor would come to the rescue, or frogs turn into handsome young men were merely deluding themselves. Such things did not happen in real life without someone making a push. Or in the middle of a conversation about something quite different, she would muse, "I wonder . . . Lord Grafton? Good family, but a widower? . . . perhaps the Earl of Wye? But only nineteen . . . tsk!"

Diana became used to her great-aunt's matchmaking, and her nods and winks whenever Diana was introduced to an eligible man at the parties they attended together. Mrs. Travis sometimes accompanied them, but more often she preferred to remain at home with her husband. The London doctor had visited, and pronounced himself satisfied with the treatment Mr. Travis had received in Eastham. He told Mrs. Travis that the pain would subside in time, and recommended a trip to Bath or Tunbridge Wells later in the month, where Mr. Travis might have the benefit of bathing in the hot springs.

Both Diana and her mother were relieved, but still Mrs.

Travis sent her daughter out more and more under the chaperonage of her great-aunt, in order to remain beside her dear Edward. Diana wondered if she herself would ever have a marriage as happy. It seemed her mother was extremely fortunate, and she could not help envying her.

Sometimes she wondered about the Duke of Clare. Was he still in London or had he returned to the Court? Not that it mattered, of course, one way or the other to her, but she could not help searching a drawing room or a theater when she first arrived, knowing his tall, powerful height would be easy to spot. When she caught herself doing this, she told herself it was only so she might be able to avoid him.

The duke was not in town. When he had arrived there and taken Lord Barrett's problems under consideration, he discovered this time Chauncy had really done it. He was being sued for breach of promise and alienation of affection. Chauncy assured Clare over and over that Miss Bagley had always known what he intended; a warm relationship unsanctioned by any religious ceremony, one that would continue as long as both parties desired it. He claimed it must be the woman's mother who was making all the fuss.

"Promise you, William, word of a Barrett! I never so much as breathed the word 'marriage.' Why, I never even walked her by a church. And Bathsheba understood—"

"Bathsheba?" the duke interrupted, somewhat startled. "Bathsheba Bagley? You have to be making that up, Chauncy."

"Bathsheba Naomi," Lord Barrett muttered. "Her mama is fond of Biblical names." As the duke began to laugh, he added defensively, "It could be a lot worse! One of her sisters is named Tirzah Salome."

When Clare could once again control himself, he said,

"The whole thing smells of the bourgeoisie to me. And how many times have you been told, Chauncy, to stick to your own kind where they understand these little affairs? I can almost picture the young lady's middle-class background. All her brothers and sisters, her scheming ma, and her chapel-going pa. All very upright and staid and conventional. How could you so forget yourself?"

He sighed in annoyance while Lord Barrett hung his head and chewed a corner of his straw-colored mustache. He was an unprepossessing young man of twenty-five, of medium height and rail thin. He had slightly protruding china-blue eyes, a high color, and straight yellow hair that was already thinning. To look at him, one would never have thought him a great rake. With his red hands and awkward gait he looked more like a fishmonger, in spite of his expensive clothes.

But Chauncy Barrett had one great mission in life, and that was to sip from as many feminine flowers as possible before age and the gout overtook him, and in pursuit of this ambition, he was persistent and single-minded, and, to be fair to the gentleman, ridiculously successful. Dowagers, debutantes, and demimondes had only to see him before their hearts were lost and they were in hot pursuit of the easily captured peer. Why, it had even been said that baby girls reached out their arms to him from their prams in the park. Clare had often wondered at his cousin's phenomenal success with the fair sex and once had gone so far as to inquire of his friend Lord Evans what he thought the fatal attraction might be.

"Haven't the foggiest, dear boy," Lord Evans had admitted, his brow furrowed in thought. "Must give off some kind of scent. Like bugs, y'know. Why, if I could bottle it, my fortune would be made!"

Now Clare realized after several sessions with the solicitors and many exchanges of letters, that he would have to travel to Glasgow, where Chauncy had met the fair Bathsheba, and dicker with her mother for his cousin's release. He sighed. It was annoying and it would cost a great deal of money, not that that mattered to Chauncy who was one of England's wealthiest men. The problem was the duke did not want to take the time. What he wanted to do was to return to Clare Court and Diana Travis as soon as possible, for no letter had come to him from her although he had been in town for some time. He was worried. He hated to leave London when the very next post might bring her reply to his pleading, heartfelt love letter, but as head of the family he had no choice. After arranging for his correspondence to be forwarded, he set out grimly for Scotland.

Once there, he promised himself he would never, under any circumstances, visit Glasgow again. Miss Bagley's mother was everything he had imagined, and much, much worse. Stout and strident, she knew she had a good thing here, and as she was also astute, would not be taken lightly. The duke also met the beautiful Bathsheba herself, and heard from her own rosebud lips, while her large violet eyes filled with dewy tears, that of course she would never . . . she certainly had been led to expect . . . she was sure he had mentioned . . . and other sentiments of like ilk that left the duke tight-lipped and angry, and Mrs. Bagley all greedy satisfaction.

At last it was settled and Clare made haste to return to town via Cuckfield. He wondered why he had not heard from Diana, and now he was free, determined to find out once and for all, what the problem was.

When he finally reached Clare Court late one afternoon, it was to discover his mother at last recovering from her fever, his sister laid down on her bed in exhaustion, and Diana Travis flown.

He had a few moments with Emily, but she could not help him.

"No traffic with the Hall, William," she said wearily. "Not with Mama so ill. Meant to write to you, but so busy. Even Cornelia shunned us, for which I for one was glad. Did hear Miss Travis had gone home—somethin' to do with her father. Sorry. Wasn't really attendin'."

Clare kissed her and ordered her to rest. At dinner that night, he told his mother in no uncertain terms that she was not to ask any services from his sister until she had regained her strength. In fact, he said, he was sending Lady Emily away on a visit to regain her health, unhampered by her mother's ceaseless demands. It was not to be expected the dowager would accept this kind of plain speaking without taking to her bed again, so it was a week before Clare was able to leave the Court, having soothed his mother's ruffled feathers, and at the same time arranged for Emily to go to her Aunt Barrett's. He also had a very interesting conversation with Cornelia, whom the dowager was quick to invite to tea on his last day at the Court.

Cornelia answered all his questions about Diana without the slightest reserve or consciousness. "Yes, she has returned to Eastham," she told him. "I suspect, my dear Clare, she has gone away to accept Roger's proposal. We are all so pleased. Such a suitable alliance for her, and better than she had any right to expect, I'm sure."

For a moment, Cornelia recalled her fury when she had heard Diana telling her sister Anne of Roger's proposal. Roger, too! It was too much to have the little snip capturing all her beaux! It served her right Cornelia had intercepted her love letter and burned it, and she was glad she had done so! She did not expect to get caught in the lies she told. The Travis family members were rare visitors to London. And if eventually it came out that Diana had not married Roger Maitland, well, it would be far too late for any punitive measures, for by then she would be the Duchess of Clare.

The duke's face darkened as the dowager chimed in, "Most suitable. I never thought to see Miss . . . Miss? make such a good match."

"Roger Maitland?" the duke asked slowly, setting his teacup down with exaggerated care.

"The very same," Cornelia assured him. "What a sly puss Diana turned out to be! She never gave anyone a hint she was busy attaching Roger."

She laughed gaily and was clever enough to turn the subject to the coming London season, and her own arrival in town within the month. The duke absently agreed he would be delighted to see her there, and when he excused himself shortly thereafter, the dowager and Cornelia had every reason to smile and nod to each other in triumphant conspiracy.

William Rawlings arrived back in town angry, confused, and deeply disappointed. So, Emily had been wrong, and he had been right after all. Of course Diana and Roger Maitland had been embracing that night in the library. But why had she lied to him—denied it? Somehow he didn't believe Diana had shown Maitland his letter, even if she did intend to marry him. At least he hoped she had not. He had been wrong about so many things lately.

But of course, her betrothal was the reason he had not heard from her. He had no idea what he was to do now. If Diana preferred Mr. Maitland, he could not force her to marry him. He felt a bleak emptiness in the pit of his stomach. To discover the girl he loved and then to lose her like this! He remembered Diana had told him she did not love him, and how her refusal to consent to becoming the Duchess of Clare would be a humbling experience for him, but he in his arrogance had not believed her. Well, he did now. And he was not only humbled, he was defeated.

Damn Chauncy and his adventures, he thought. If it had not taken so much time to extricate his cousin from his amorous tangle, he might have been able to reach Diana and change her mind. Now it was much too late for that.

The duke was very abrupt with his overly obsequious servants that evening, and he only toyed with his excellent dinner. He also sent a message to Lord Evans canceling an engagement before he retired to his library with a bottle of old brandy to keep him company in his misery.

Not more than half a mile away, if he had but known it, Miss Diana Travis was curtsying to that same Lord Evans, who had decided to attend the reception being given without Clare after all. Diana wondered if she should ask for the duke, just to be polite, for she knew Lord Evans was one of his closest friends.

Lady Michaels hurried her along before she could do so. She whispered that although Pierpont Evans came from excellent stock, it was well known he would be wise to marry money, so there was no sense in her great-niece wasting either her smiles or her time on the man.

8

If he had only gone to that reception, or if his friend had only thought to mention he had seen Miss Travis there, the duke might not have been so stunned a few evenings later when he entered the ballroom of Lady Martin's town house on Park Lane and came face to face with the young lady herself.

"*You!*" she whispered, her face white with shock.

"*What? You* here, Diana?" he asked in disbelief.

This was so unusual an exchange that Lady Michaels, resplendent in purple silk, perked up immediately from her position at Diana's elbow. If she was not mistaken, she told herself, a Roman candle was about to be set off.

But Diana had no intention of satisfying her great-aunt on this occasion. Curtsying as shallowly as she dared, she begged His Grace to excuse her. Without waiting for his reply, she marched away with her head held high and her determined little chin firmly set. Lady Michaels was forced to follow her, leaving the duke with a red face, and the hand he had extended so imploringly to fall empty at his side.

He longed to follow her, to speak to her or ask her to dance, but of course he knew he could not do that. She would only cut him if he dared. Thinking hard, he realized she had probably come to town to purchase her bride clothes. He looked around the ballroom for Roger Maitland, but was not encouraged when he did not see him. It wasn't at all necessary for the future bridegroom to dance attendance on his bride at this time. Indeed, he would only be very much in the way when the lady had her mind on silks and muslins, bonnets and nightrobes, and the important decision of whether her wedding gown should be made of silk or lace.

From her chair across the room, Diana refused to look his way. He saw her aunt whispering to her in great animation, and he also saw Diana's brief reply. Lady Michaels was forced to subside but she promised herself she would get to the bottom of this somehow—and soon! She wondered if Sarah and Edward had any idea . . . my word, the Duke of Clare! This was even better than she had hoped.

Lady Michaels was not disappointed when Clare did not come near Diana again, nor was she in the least surprised to see him leave the ball at a very early hour, and without dancing with anyone. Diana, she was pleased to see, never lacked a partner and was very animated. She laughed at all the gentlemen's sallies and appeared to be having a wonderful time. And, Lady Michaels told herself, surely I am the only one who noticed how the gel reverted to her usual quiet behavior as soon as the duke took himself off.

Diana was furious at herself. After all the time she had watched for him, she had never imagined she would betray herself so obviously the first time she came face to face with him. And there was her great-aunt's curiosity to satisfy as well. But now she knew he was in town, there would be no repeat of such a contretemps. She would be cold, and only as polite as good manners demanded.

Once again pacing his library, Clare was deciding on a

similar course. The lady was promised to another. She did not want him. She need have no fear he would embarrass her with unwanted attentions, for if he had nothing else, at least he still had his pride. Icy correctness would be his watchword from now on. He resolved to look up Lady Cornelia as soon as she arrived in town. His mother had written that the lady would be traveling with the dowager Lady Stafford, although the viscount and his bride were not expected to attend the season this year, due to her interesting condition. Clare could almost hear his mother's wistful sigh as she penned this bit of news, and he was delighted she had decided to remain at the Court a few weeks longer.

London society was not so large that the duke and Diana could avoid each other indefinitely. They met at various social occasions, each hewing to their predetermined course. Lady Michaels was forced to admit that perhaps Clare had not tendered one of Di's two proposals, and there were some among the ton who wondered why Miss Travis had taken such a handsome catch in aversion. They were not enlightened. A bow, a curtsy, a stilted phrase were all that were exchanged, although one afternoon at a picnic at Richmond, the duke found himself beside Diana and could not resist asking for Roger Maitland. Diana raised one brow.

"Roger, sir? He is at home in Littledean. I am sure we are all looking forward to his arrival in town, however."

"I am sure you *especially* must be," the duke snapped before he left her abruptly.

Puzzled, Diana watched him stride away. She wondered what on earth he had meant. Was he still remembering the scene in the library at Clare Court? But why should that continue to bother him when he was about to marry Cornelia?

In due course, the lady posted up to town with all her trunks and boxes, and in her aunt's company. It was not very long before the ton was predicting her imminent engagement to the Duke of Clare. He was so very attentive and so much in her company, the odds in the clubs were running strongly in La Cornelia's favor.

Cornelia almost purred with satisfaction for it was all working out just as she had planned. She accompanied her aunt on a call to Lady Michaels where she was reunited with Diana, to neither lady's unmitigated delight. Cornelia did not think Diana looked well, even in her smart London gowns, but she was not moved to suggest the girl smile more and at least try to appear content. To add insult to injury, she even mentioned William Rawlings with such regularity that Diana was glad when they finally took their leave, fond as she was of the dowager Lady Stafford. That good woman took her niece to task on their drive home.

"It was most unwise of you, Cornelia, to show your ambition so plain," she said. "There's many a slip between courtship and the altar, so have a care! After all, though Clare has known you a long time, he has not asked you to marry him yet, now has he?"

Cornelia admitted he had not, but informed her aunt in a smug little voice that it was only a matter of time now. Lady Stafford sighed and wished she could like her sister-in-law's child more.

More of the quality were arriving in town every day, and it was not long before the dowager duchess herself was ensconced at Clare House in Eaton Square, and reunited with her daughter. Lady Emily, after two weeks of complete rest at her Aunt Barrett's, was in fine fettle again. She confided to her brother on her first evening home when the dowager had gone out to dine with friends, that she had forgotten how wonderful it was not to have to think of anyone but herself—such luxury! Clare was chagrined he had never thought to suggest she have regular respites from her dear mama before, for Emily was not a slave! When he told her he was going to insist on it from now on, she smiled.

"But don't mention it to Mama just yet, William," she said. "Always better in town. Has so many amusements here I'm seldom expected to be at her beck and call. What news of Miss Travis?" she added, changing the subject abruptly in her usual way.

Her brother's face was grim. "You were wrong, Em. Miss Travis is engaged to Roger Maitland. I discovered it before I came up to town, but I did not like to tell you when you were feeling so pulled."

"Very sorry to hear it. Who told you?"

"Why, Cornelia. Serves me right, eh? The arrogant Duke of Clare is vanquished at last." He laughed bitterly, and in turn changed the subject. His sister followed his lead. It was disappointing news, for she liked Miss Travis and felt she would have been the perfect wife for her dear brother. She only hoped he would continue to avoid ensnarement by Cornelia.

But the duke was not even bothering to do this. After all, he told himself, if he could not have Diana, what difference did it make who he married? And Cornelia looked like a duchess. In fact he was sure she would make an admirable one since she wanted the position so badly. And if she was cold—frigid, really—well, that did not matter to him either. In fact, he preferred it for he knew he would never have been able to marry a girl who adored him and expected him to love her in return. He had no love left to give to anyone else. Diana had it all.

But still he did not ask the fatal question, even though

Cornelia and all London society waited for him to do so. Something held him back, something that stilled his tongue every time he had the opportunity, and trust Cornelia to arrange a number of those!

The duke continued to watch Diana flirting with the beaux she had assembled around her, and he thought cynically that if he had been Roger Maitland he would have sent them packing and taken his betrothed away from town in a minute, lecturing her on her behavior all the while.

He was driving Cornelia in Hyde Park one afternoon at the fashionable hour all society gathered to chat and stroll and drive, and chanced to see Diana walking with the Follett brothers. He nodded as his carriage passed them, his expression bleak. Cornelia smiled and waved.

"I'm surprised Maitland allows Diana to see so many other men," he remarked somewhat savagely.

"Why, what's the harm, Clare?" Cornelia asked, her big brown eyes wide. "Surely there is no danger from Harold and Robert Follett—besides, safety in numbers, you know."

"But only last evening she waltzed twice with Percy Nottingham. You can't say Sir Percy is safe!"

Lady Cornelia sighed inwardly. Clare was still being tiresome about Diana. She saw she would have to take steps, and she ran her hand caressingly up and down his arm.

"My dear Clare," she murmured, "do not think me bold, but would it be possible for us to be private? There is something . . . I mean, I must tell you . . . please, dear Clare?"

"We're private now," he said, bowing to Lady Jersey and her party.

Cornelia fumed until he turned and smiled down at her,

then she pouted. "With all London watching us? No, I mean *completely* private," she said.

Her hand tightened on his arm and Clare was hard put to control his team. "Steady, Cornelia," he told her. "These horses are new to town and unreliable."

Behind them, his groom curled his lip in disgust at such a silly female.

Clare completed a circuit of the park, but when he did not see Diana and her escorts again, he came to a decision and halted the team. The groom went to their heads.

"Very well, we'll walk for a bit, Cornelia, while you tell me what's on your mind. Hold 'em, Tom."

The groom nodded and tugged his cap, snickering a little to himself. As if anyone with half a brain wouldn't know what the lady was up to!

Cornelia barely waited until they were out of sight of the carriageway before she pretended to stumble over a pebble in the path. She clutched the duke's arm as if she were about to fall. Clare put his arm around her to steady her, and she turned toward him, molding herself against him. She raised her face to his, parting her lips in invitation and murmuring, "Clare!" in her husky, deceiving voice.

The duke was more than half-amused at her tactics, but looking down at her beautiful face with its soft, full lips and half-closed eyes, he decided the time had come at last, and he bent to kiss her. Cornelia felt a surge of triumph, and she opened her lips in an imitation of desire as his mouth took possession of hers. His strong hands caressed her hips and back, pulling her closer still. To Cornelia the kiss was endless, but she steeled herself not only to endure it, but return it with equal ardor.

When the duke raised his head at last, she was panting, but there was no way he could know it was from disgust.

"Why, Cornelia, you surprise me," he murmured, somewhat taken back at her expertise and passion. He continued to caress her, and although she longed to escape his touch, the lady had herself in firm control.

"My darling, what an age it has taken you to kiss me! I can't tell you how I have longed for your touch," she said. She kept her eyes closed for she could not bear to look at him, disgusting man that he was to be pawing her this way!

"Marry me," Clare commanded in his deep, harsh voice.

At that her eyes flew open and she nodded. "But of course I will, my dear. I have been waiting to do so forever." Her voice was demure, but then she put her head back and laughed her satisfaction. The duke, looking over her shoulder, saw Diana Travis and her escorts standing a little distance away, watching them. Diana had one hand to her lips and her hazel eyes looked stunned. It was obvious she had seen everything that had happened. As he stared at her, she whirled and hurried away, followed by the Folletts, both identically red. He had a sudden urge to call out to Diana, tell her to wait, for he could explain everything. Then reason returned, and in a moment she was gone. Cornelia did not even suspect they had been observed, it had all happened so fast.

Clare's face twisted in agony for a moment before he pulled Cornelia close again and subjected her to yet another searing kiss. Why, he wondered, why did I have to see Diana just then? Why be forced to recall how different her kisses had been from his newly betrothed? Diana had been shy yet eager, and her mouth had trembled under his, but even so he had been able to tell the exact moment when she had begun to respond to him and kiss him back. Compared to her, Cornelia had all the spontaneity of a streetwalker with her practiced ecstasy. Savagely he explored her open mouth with his tongue, and she stiffened and pulled away from him, her face white.

"Clare, you must not . . . I cannot bear it!" At his frown and uplifted brows, she steadied herself and added weakly, "I must beg you for more time to become accustomed, before allowing you such . . . such intimacies."

The duke apologized, feeling a little ashamed of himself. Obviously Cornelia was not very experienced after all, in spite of her veneer of sophistication. When he tried to take her in his arms again for a gentle caress, she put her hands on his chest and held him off.

"No, no more!" she cried.

He thought she sounded on the edge of hysteria and would have reassured her, except she was soon in control of herself again. Straightening her bonnet and gown, she suggested they return to the phaeton. "I'm sure I look a perfect fright and everyone will know what we've been doing," she said, hurrying down the path. He noticed she did not stumble now.

"But of course they will," he agreed, trying to smile warmly. "Just as soon as our engagement is announced. Did you think they would not, my dear? But all betrothed couples take part in such delights as often as they can."

Cornelia blushed and tried not to shudder. To think everyone in the haut ton would know; it was too embarrassing! And that she—the Lady Cornelia—had been subjected to such indignities, to realize there would be more of them, with even more passion, even greater liberties taken with her person! For a moment, her courage failed, and she almost begged to be excused from the engagement. Then she remembered she was to be the

Duchess of Clare. For that, she told herself, she would put up with a great deal.

As the duke helped her to her seat in his phaeton, she resolved never to be alone with him any more than she could help, and to delay the wedding date for as long as possible as well. The duke's groom smirked at her and she blushed and sent him a look of pure loathing. Another *male* . . . and he knew!

But by the time the duke climbed up, took the reins, and motioned to Tom to let 'em go!, she was calm and able to smile at him while they discussed the wording of the announcement Clare said he would send to the journals that very day. She did, however, insist he take her home at once, even though he offered to drive her to Clare House so she might tell the dowager herself of their engagement. She excused herself by saying she wanted to rest so she might look her best for him that evening at Lady Evans's soiree. In reality, she was afraid the duchess would not be at home, and she'd be left alone with him and his disgusting passion once again.

When they parted, she was delighted Clare only kissed her hand, and did not seem to want to come in with her. Hand kissing was permissible, even enjoyable. Everything else connected with engagements was dirty and sordid, she thought as she hurried to her room to wash her face and thoroughly rinse her mouth.

When Clare announced his betrothal that evening at dinner, the dowager beamed with happiness. But Emily, although she tried to appear content for his sake, could not quite conceal her dismay that he had succumbed to Cornelia's wiles at last.

"Dearest boy, the wish of my heart! So happy," his mother enthused. "You must send to the Court for the ancestral betrothal ring, and at once. How lovely Cornelia will look wearing that huge emerald with its diamond surround."

For some reason, Clare found himself rebelling, for in his mind that was still Diana's ring. "I think not, Mother. I intend to buy Cornelia a more modern token. I've never liked that old setting and do not think it would become her hand."

"Perhaps a large white, icy diamond would be appropriate," Lady Emily murmured.

"Careful, Em," the duke said, and she subsided.

The announcement duly appeared in all the papers, and congratulations and best wishes poured in. Cornelia was in her element, as long as Clare only stood beside her, a handsome consort, and she was not forced to endure anything more than a chaste kiss at the end of an evening. The duke seemed to have lost interest in any more passionate embraces, for which she was extremely thankful. She enjoyed all the trappings of their betrothal, the parties given in their honor, the smiles and nods when they danced together, and she adored the enormous diamond he bought her and placed on her hand. She even delighted in visiting Clare House and planning how she would redecorate it, and Clare Court as well, as soon as they were married and she had relegated the duke's dreary mother and tiresome sister to the dower house.

Many wagers were settled in Brooks and Whites, and Pierpont Evans told the duke he hoped he realized that by proposing to the Lady Cornelia, he had cost his friend a large sum of money. "I was so sure you would never come up to scratch, Clare," he grieved. "Put down all my blunt on it. Whoever would have thought you'd succumb to La Cornelia . . . my word! Gorgeous, of course, but . . . would have said it was impossible."

Lord Barrett was even more confounded. "Here now,

cuz, do consider what you've gone and done! Mean to say, early days yet. Years before you need set up your nursery. Yes, I know she's a beauty, but to be tied to only one when the world is full of 'em! Think what you'll be missin'!"

Clare ignored them both. He had an uneasy feeling he had done something not only rash but dire, but there was no getting out of it now. It was almost like riding a runaway horse over which he had no control, so he was forced to go where the horse wanted, even if it meant going to his doom. Then he would shrug and try to dismiss such ridiculous thoughts. He had made a commitment, and of course he would honor it.

He did not see Diana Travis for some time for she had sent her regrets to the Evans's ball, and all the rest of the week's festivities. When Lady Michaels and her mother tried to discover why, she said she was overtired from the many parties and late nights. Lady Michaels would have probed deeper, but Mrs. Travis, catching sight of Diana's pale face and the tears lurking in her eyes, as well as the way she twisted her hands in her skirts, took her aunt firmly away.

"But, Sarah," Lady Michaels protested, as soon as they were alone, "what's amiss with Di?"

"I'm not entirely sure, but knowing my daughter and her moods, I know it will be better to leave her alone until she is in better spirits. Something must have happened, but I've no idea what it could be."

It was not long before they had more than an inkling after the duke's engagement was announced and Lady Stafford came to call to discuss it with them.

"To tell you the truth, I never thought Cornelia would pull it off," this lady declared, after the butler had brought a tea tray and bowed himself from the room.

Mrs. Travis nodded, and encouraged, Lady Staffor
continued, "I could have sworn there was somethin
afoot between Clare and Diana when we were all a
Cuckfield. Anne thought so as well."

"Never say so," Lady Michaels exclaimed before sh
told them of the scene she had witnessed when the duk
and her great-niece had met in London for the first time

After half an hour of gossip and speculation, Mrs
Travis sighed. "There is nothing more to be said. I mus
admit that I myself thought the duke was attracted to D
when I first met him at the Abbey. Of course I did no
mention that to Edward."

The other two ladies nodded in complete understand
ing as she went on, "That is why I sent her to Staffor
Hall, of course. But if the duke prefers Lady Cornelia
that must be the end of it, no matter how unhappy Dian
is."

She changed the subject, and Lady Michaels wa
forced to swallow all the things she had been about to say
She did not forget them, however. Clare was only en
gaged, not married. There were a lot of things that coul
be done, and if Sarah was too staid and conventional t
see to it, she would do it herself.

Accordingly, she went to Diana's room the followin
morning as soon as she knew the girl was awake. Sh
found her sitting up in bed, staring out the window look
ing miserable. Lady Michaels drew a deep breath as sh
took a chair beside the bed and charged into battle.

"So, you intend to remain in this room for the rest o
the season, do you, gel?" she asked, shaking her finger a
Diana. "I thought you had more courage than that."

As Diana only stared, she added, "I know everything
Do not try to dissemble with me, miss! Besides, there ar
other fish in the sea, and one duke is not the world, yo

know. And how can you let that snippety Lady Cornelia have the satisfaction of knowing she has vanquished you so thoroughly? Put up your head, gel! Remember your name!"

For a moment, Diana hung her head instead. She had come to see that one particular duke *was* the world—her world at least. But it was too late. Oh, why had she kept putting him off? Why hadn't she confessed she loved him when she had the chance?

Lady Michaels watched her face carefully. "Of course it's obvious you don't care for the duke as much as I suspected, for if you did, you'd make more of a push to get him back. I suppose you'll be off to Crompton Abbey with your parents next week, and all the time I thought you had more spunk!"

"I do *so* care for him," Diana was stung into replying, "but what good does it do? He's engaged to Cornelia, and you don't know Clare if you think he'd go back on his word."

Lady Michaels hid her satisfaction at this disclosure. "Pooh, my girl, I say 'pooh'! There's no stigma attached to a broken engagement if it's the lady who terminates it."

"But Cornelia *wants* to marry him! She's been chasing him forever," Diana wailed.

"That may be, but there are ways, you know. Well, no, you don't, but I do, which is more to the point. I'll think on this. For now, you're going to get up and get dressed for we are going shopping. I'm going to buy you the most beautiful gown in London. That will perk up your spirits! And then the next time you see Clare and Cornelia, you will smile and smile and *smile*. And you'll wish them happy with all the ease you can muster. Then you're to captivate all the hearts you can, and you will not retreat to the country—you will not continue to cut the duke in that stupid way you have been doing—and *then* we shall see!"

The old lady nodded as she struggled to her feet. "Believe me, Di, you must never say 'die.' Aha, I made a joke! And I'll be with you to help, you know, and I've many a trick up this old sleeve . . ." She nodded again and winked, and Diana was forced to chuckle weakly. She knew there was nothing to be done, but it was plain to see her great-aunt didn't believe that. She supposed she would have to be humored, for she did, after all, mean well.

And so Miss Diana Travis again appeared in company, beautifully gowned and coiffed, with her head held high and a glittering smile on her face. When Lord Evans began to pay her some attention, Lady Michaels even encouraged him. "He is a great friend of the duke's, and a handsome scamp as well. We'll make use of him."

The Follett brothers were delighted to see Diana again, Sir Percy Nottingham was most attentive, and Lady Michaels beamed when a Lord Cole joined Diana's growing list of beaux.

She was able to say good-bye to her niece with confidence when the Travises left town. "Never fear, Sarah," she whispered as Diana kissed her father once more, "I have all in hand. You may depend on me."

Mrs. Travis tried to look suitably appreciative, but she prayed all the way back to Crompton Abbey that her Aunt Emma would restrain herself and not make things any worse than they were right now. She had had a long talk with Diana, and the girl seemed more resigned to the loss of the duke now, and even appeared to be regaining her spirits. Mrs. Travis hoped her daughter's good sense would temper any wild starts of her Aunt Emma's, and although she wished she might remain on the scene to make sure, her husband was anxious to return home, and she could not let him go alone.

It was on the evening after her parents' departure that Diana finally saw the duke and his intended at Almacks. She had been talking to Lord Evans, and since Lady Jersey had given her permission to waltz, she was happy to agree to the next dance. As the young man took her in his arms, she saw a glowing Cornelia enter the room on the duke's arm. For a moment, her step faltered, but when Lord Evans was quick to apologize for his clumsiness, she put the two new arrivals from her mind, and smiled and laughed and flirted until the dance was over.

Then her heart sank into her satin slippers when she saw the duke beckon to Lord Evans, and she wished her partner was not so quick to obey his summons and lead her to where Clare and Cornelia were standing.

"*Dearest* Di"—Cornelia greeted her with a warm, caressing smile—"I hear you have been ill—how very unfortunate. I hope it was nothing serious, although I do seem to remember someone saying you had a . . . mm . . . heart ailment?"

Diana's temper rose, and this steadied her so she was able to say easily, "How absurd! As you can see, there is nothing wrong with my heart. But forgive me—this is the first opportunity I've had. Your Grace, Cornelia . . . allow me to wish you both happy."

Clare had not taken his eyes from Diana's face, a fact Cornelia noted as she moved closer to him and took his arm. The large diamond ring she wore glinted in the light as she nodded complacently.

"Thank you," the duke said, his harsh voice serious and not a hint of a smile on his handsome face. Diana turned aside a little to fan herself. A set was forming, and

Lord Evans, knowing he could not ask Diana to dance with him again so soon, begged the privilege of leading Lady Cornelia to the floor. She did not want to leave Clare and Diana alone together, but the duke spoke up before she could refuse.

"Do indulge Pierpont, my dear. It will give me an opportunity to admire how graceful you are."

Lady Cornelia threw a triumphant smile Diana's way, and somewhat reassured, took Lord Evans's arm. Clare indicated a sofa nearby.

"Will you sit with me a while and talk, Miss Travis?" he asked.

Diana looked around for an approaching partner, then studied her dance card. Unfortunately she was not engaged until the next set, and there was no way she could refuse without being discourteous. Out of the corner of her eye she saw her great-aunt who was seated some distance away with her companion, making shooing motions of encouragement with her fan. Afraid the duke might see her also, and wonder what she was up to, she nodded.

She could not think of a single thing to say, so she stared at the couples dancing and tried to calm her rapid heartbeat. Clare studied her profile for a moment, then, finding the silence as awkward as she did, said, "Mr. Maitland has not arrived in town as yet? I find it difficult to believe he could stay away so long; I am sure I could not."

Diana smiled, but she only looked in his eyes a fleeting moment, lest he see more in her face than she cared to reveal. Lowering her gaze to the gold sticks of her fan, she replied, "Perhaps his father has had a reoccurrence of the gout, sir. Or there might be estate matters—"

"You mean *you* don't know why he hasn't come?" Clare asked, his voice incredulous.

"I don't know why I should," Diana answered, much perplexed.

"Well, here's a new come-out indeed! I never thought to see you so meek, Diana, not to take exception to such neglect."

Diana stared at him now. He had sounded so indignant, but she didn't for the life of her understand why.

"As to that, Your Grace, I'm sure I'm not so conceited I think every man must be constantly bombarding me with attentions."

"But surely Roger Maitland is not just *any* man," the duke persisted.

"Of course not. I am very fond of him," Diana replied with composure even as she wondered what Great-Aunt Emma would make of this conversation. For herself, she felt she was going mad—or the duke was.

He snorted. "How delighted I am to hear you say so, beauty. Of course there must be fondness, at the very least, don't you agree? But why did you feel you had to settle for that, when a great deal more was offered you?"

He sounded as perplexed as she felt, and not knowing how to answer him, she turned to study the dancers again.

"I was disappointed not to hear from you after I left the Court, Diana," he said next, and although she was delighted with the change of subject, Diana did not feel this topic would be any more illuminating than his last.

"I can't imagine why you expected you would, sir," she said, still refusing to meet his eye again.

He put his hand on her arm, but before he could ask why she denied receiving his love letter, she pulled free.

Her face was pale—so was his. He heard the music coming to an end, and knowing he had just a few moments before Cornelia returned, he said quickly, "Look at me, Di, I beg of you!"

Reluctantly, those wide-spaced hazel eyes met his, and he saw a tear sparkling in her dark lashes. "I know I should not touch you. It is not my right. But may I say how very much I regret it?" he said.

Diana gasped. How could he pretend the sadness she heard in his voice? Was no act of seduction too vile for him, even now? "*You* regret it? But you have already made your choice, sir, the choice everyone, myself included, expected you to make."

He could see she was losing her temper and put out his hand in warning but she continued in a quick, breathy whisper, "I knew all along you would marry Cornelia. You didn't fool me with your wild statements and teasing words about love. Duchess of Clare, indeed! I'm glad I'm not some impressionable little miss, for if I had been so foolish as to take you at your word, I would be heartbroken now. But rakes are such notorious liars, are they not? I understand, even though I do most thoroughly condemn you for your deceit!"

She wanted to tell him how much she despised him. She wanted to ask him how he could make love to her when all along he was planning to marry Cornelia. She wanted to rant and rail at him, pummel him with her fists, but remembering her great-aunt's warning, she only added, "We have indulged in a pleasant flirtation, have we not, Your Grace? But you must agree it is over now."

There was no time for any more, for Cornelia and Lord Evans arrived and they were forced to chat of innocuous things until Sir Percy Nottingham came to claim his dance with Diana.

As she rose from her curtsy, Sir Percy and Lord Evans were exchanging a few private words, and Lady Cornelia had turned aside to speak to a friend for a moment, so Clare took the opportunity to whisper, "It may be over, but it was no flirtation. I did not lie to you, Diana, I loved you."

Diana stared at him in shock and he gave her a twisted travesty of a smile.

"I am sorry you could not return that love, more sorry than you will ever know, but may I, in turn, wish *you* happy, too?"

9

Sir Percy Nottingham, an accomplished man-about-town, well known for his wit and neat turn of phrase, would have been astounded if he had known the fascinating, lovely Miss Travis did not hear a word he said to her during their dance in Almacks Rooms that night. Diana managed to smile and laugh in all the right places, and she had discovered how helpful it was when you were not attending to your partner, to say whenever he paused, "How very interesting," or "How droll!" if he were laughing himself. Yet all the while, your mind and heart and soul never left the tall man across the room.

By the time Sir Percy returned Diana to her great-aunt, he was satisfied he was making great progress with her, and he preened a little as he greeted the elderly lady.

"Run along, Percy, do," she said, waving her fan in dismissal as if he were no more than two and ten. But of course she had known him since infancy and had sent a silver rattle for his christening, so there was no way he could take offense at such cavalier treatment. "You may come back later, if you wish, but for now, I must speak to Diana alone."

As Sir Percy strolled away after a last, burning glance of regret for Diana, Lady Michaels whispered, "Not that I have any intention of speaking to you here and now, Di, but I could see you needed some time to recover from your tête-à-tête with the duke. Smile, gel! Lady Cornelia is looking this way."

Diana obeyed, but her great-aunt hoped La Cornelia's eyesight was not too keen for she herself had never seen such a weak imitation of enjoyment. Diana whispered she wished they could go home at once, but this Lady Michaels refused to consider since she had no intention of allowing the duke's betrothed to feel she had routed Diana. She explained this to the girl, saying they would leave at midnight and not a moment before.

So Diana was forced to dance again with Sir Percy, Lord Evans, and Lord Cole who had been so adroit as to secure her hand for the final waltz. It seemed an age to her before her great-aunt announced she was tired and wished to leave, if Diana did not mind forgoing the remainder of this delightful evening. Sending Diana's admirers packing, she instructed her companion not to forget her shawl, her reticule, and her fan, before she swept from the rooms with Diana and Polly in tow, and they all went out to where the carriage waited for them in King Street.

At home, she issued a stream of orders as she headed for the library. The butler was to make up the fire and then fetch them a large pot of tea, Polly was to hustle off to bed since she was so tongue-tied she would be of no use at all during their discussion, and Diana was instructed to take off her stole and gloves and make herself comfortable. As for Lady Michaels, she intended to remove the devilish tight slippers that had pained her all evening.

At last all was accomplished, and Lady Michaels settled down in a comfortable armchair and propped her feet up on a footstool so she might wriggle her pinched toes before she commanded, "Start at the very beginning and tell me everything he said to you."

"Well, first he asked me to sit out the dance with him so we might talk, after Lord Evans took Cornelia away to dance," Diana said obediently.

"What was the first, the very first thing he said after you were seated?" Lady Michaels asked eagerly, before she blew on her tea to cool it.

"He asked me why Roger Maitland had not come to town, almost as if he expected *me* to know all about Roger's activities," Diana said, her brow wrinkled with thought.

Lady Michaels was bewildered. "But who on earth is this Roger Maitland, pray tell, and what does he have to say to anything?" she asked, sounding almost discouraged at this less than promising beginning.

Diana explained the relationship, and her great-aunt waved a dismissing hand. "I can't make any sense of it, but go on. It may be clearer later."

Diana stared into the fire, her tea forgotten. "I don't understand what the duke meant myself. We seemed to be talking at cross purposes. He said something about there should be 'fondness at the very least,' and he wondered why I had settled for only that—we were still discussing Roger then, you see. I wonder what he meant?"

Lady Michaels sighed. "Did you discuss nothing but this boring Maitland person?" she asked before she took another slurpy sip of her tea.

"Mostly, but then he said he was disappointed he had not heard from me after he left the Court." She sniffed and added, "As if I would write to him or any man even if he wrote to me first!"

Lady Michaels sat up straighter. "Pour me another cup of tea, Di—no, I'll have a brandy. At last there is something we can get our teeth into. But I think you had better go back to the very beginning first. How did you meet Clare? Tell me everything, and don't leave a single thing out."

Diana complied, speaking for several uninterrupted minutes. Her voice faltered sometimes, but she knew instinctively that her great-aunt would not be shocked by the account, as her mother might have been. Lady Michaels came from an earlier generation that had delighted in calling a spade a spade, and she was still very much a woman of the world.

At the end of Diana's story, the old lady crowed. "I see—oh, yes, I see—I am beginning to see at last!" She waved her brandy snifter and bounced up and down in her chair in her excitement. "Oh, why weren't there any men like Clare about when I was young?" she mourned. "Such élan . . . such style! But continue, Di. Tell me exactly what happened at Stafford Hall the day the duke left Cuckfield."

Diana sipped her tea to ease her tired throat. "It was just an ordinary day. I had breakfast with Anne and we worked on our needlepoint for a while. Then we went upstairs to dress for a loo party at— Oh, I remember now! It wasn't an ordinary day at all and in the end we never did get to the party because that was the day Gregory was shot."

"Gregory was shot? What excitin' lives people lead in the country these days! Now I've always found rural locations boring. Who is, or *was,* Gregory?"

Diana explained and Lady Michaels's eyes narrowed as she sat deep in thought. For several minutes there was no sound in the room except for the ticking of the grandfather clock, and the soft noises the fire made in the grate.

"I've got it, I'm *sure* I've got it," she said at last, bouncing so vigorously the plumes on her turban trembled as it in a high breeze. Diana jumped, startled by her sudden excitement.

"Listen, Di, my good, intelligent gel, and tell me how this strikes you. Clare posts off—*rapidimente!*—on some urgent family matter no doubt, and since he has no time to see you, he leaves a letter which is brought over to the Hall that morning. Lady Stafford's butler is just about to bring it to you when—*voilá!*—the wounded Gregory appears, confusion reigns, the family and servants hurry to his aid. There is noise, hysteria, blood—of course the letter is forgotten in the general excitement. But *someone* sees it, my, yes—*someone* who recognizes the duke's handwriting. And that *someone* picks it up and hides it. *Someone* whose name is—"

"Cornelia!" Diana chimed in. Then she covered her mouth with both hands, looking shocked.

"But that is much too fanciful, ma'am! Even Cornelia would not . . ." Her voice died away as she realized from what she knew of that lady, she most certainly would.

"You see if I'm not right, Di," Lady Michaels said, proud of her reasoning. "And Clare, when you do not even reply to his words of love—ah, how I wish I might have seen that letter!—thinks you do not care for him, especially after you cut him the first time he meets you in town. Since he must marry somebody, he then proposes to Lady Cornelia. She made sure she was available by being constantly in his company."

"Cornelia did mention to me the day after the ball that she and the duke had shared a good laugh at my expense. She even warned me not to take him too seriously. How infamous! I could scratch her eyes out!"

Lady Michaels chuckled. "Let's hope it doesn't come to that, Di, not that she doesn't deserve it. Now," the old lady added, a militant look in her eyes, "all we have to do is tell Clare and he'll break the engagement and propose to you."

"No, he won't," Diana corrected her. "He'll never go back on his offer. What, the Duke of Clare put Lady Cornelia in such an embarrassing position? Never! He's a gentleman. Besides, all this is only a theory of yours. We can't prove it, and *she'll* never admit it even if it is true."

"You're right. She's as shrewd as she can hold together, is La Cornelia," her great-aunt agreed. "But there must be some way . . ."

"And she's so beautiful too, isn't she?" Diana asked mournfully. "Who would believe such treachery of her?"

"So is a tiger beautiful," Lady Michaels snapped, "and it doesn't behave as it ought to either!"

They discussed the situation for several more minutes, Diana pleading with her great-aunt not to tell the duke as she threatened to do. At last Lady Michaels agreed, albeit reluctantly. Changing the subject before Diana could think to extract her promise, she asked, "What did the duke say at the very end, Di? Tell me word for word if you can remember."

Diana spoke very softly. "He said, 'It may be over, but it was no flirtation. I did not lie to you. I loved you, and I am sorry you could not return that love.' "

Lady Michaels paused in the act of putting her slippers back on so she might go up to bed. "Now that is the best thing I've heard all night, because you see, he loves you still."

"But he said something after that, I remember," Diana continued. "He said he must wish me happy, too."

Lady Michaels shook her head. "I am too tired to figure that out, dear Di. Was he being sarcastic because of all your beaux? It doesn't seem like him, somehow. Perhaps he had heard some rumor . . . from Cornelia even?" She sighed and added, "Come, Di, let's go to bed. Perhaps tomorrow we'll understand it better, but in any event, it is all most encouraging, besides being the most fun I've had in years. Rockets and salutes galore!"

There was someone else who kept late hours that evening. The duke, after taking Cornelia back to Lady Stafford's, forgot he had an engagement to play cards with some friends in London's latest hell, and went home to ponder his conversation with Diana instead. Why had she behaved so casually about her fiancé? he wondered. And why had she as much as denied receiving his letter? The duke knew any order of his was instantly obeyed. There was no chance that letter had not been delivered to Stafford Hall first thing in the morning. It was not even worth checking for she must have received it. And why did she insist they had only been flirting with each other when he had told her over and over that he loved her?

Since the duke did not have Lady Michaels at his elbow, he did not reach any satisfactory answers to his speculations, and when he took himself off to bed much later, he was still in a quandary, convinced there was no understanding women at all. Talk about enigmas! Besides, he was engaged to Cornelia now. There was nothing he could do about the bewitching and bothersome Miss Travis. As she herself had reminded him, she was not for him anymore.

Whenever they chanced to meet in the days that followed, the duke was cool but correct, and Diana distant but polite. One of the more uncomfortable evenings Diana spent was when she and her great-aunt attended a gala at Vauxhall as the guests of Lord Cole.

As Diana took her seat in the gaily decorated booth

Lord Cole had reserved for his party, she looked up to find herself facing the Duke of Clare in the booth directly opposite. With him were his mother, his sister, Pierpont Evans, an elderly gentleman Diana did not recognize, and of course, his fiancée, Cornelia. Catching sight of her, that lady waved gaily, and even went so far as to blow a kiss.

Lady Michaels poked her with her fan and whispered, "Thou shalt not kill! How unfortunate God placed that commandment on us. In this instance I'd be delighted to assist you, m'dear."

Diana smiled thinly to Cornelia, but that smile broadened for Lady Emily who was also waving. She noticed Cornelia whispering to the dowager, who raised her pince-nez, no doubt to more closely inspect Miss . . . Miss? Finally Diana was forced to look at the duke, and she saw those piercing hazel eyes of his boring right through her as if he wanted to read her mind.

She was quick to turn away to chat with Lord Cole and the other guests, and she resolved to ignore the duke and his party for the rest of the evening.

Her great-aunt had no such compunctions, and Diana was forced to take her to task finally, for she was being very obvious. She never took her eyes from the booth across the way, not even when the famous burnt ham shavings, the tiny biscuits, and the excellent champagne were served at midnight.

"For heavens sake, ma'am," Diana hissed in her ear. "They'll know they're being watched! Do try to attend to our party, if you please. Your behavior is making me so uncomfortable."

Lady Michaels dropped her eyes at last. Under cover of the others' conversation, she said, "Oh, very well, but I find them most unusual. I would never believe a newly engaged couple could be so casual together. I can only assume all is not going well with them, and isn't that grand? That doesn't surprise me as far as Clare is concerned, but why is Cornelia so distant? She's hardly smiled at him, or spoken, and she certainly hasn't touched him. In my experience, most engaged couples don't seem to be able to keep their hands off each other, even in public. But those two . . . one might suppose they'd been married for years, and just before coming out tonight, had had a roaring argument over the size of the lady's dress bill. Now, why should this be?"

Diana was not at all sure the elderly lady might not climb over the low railing at the front of the booth, stalk across the way, and demand an answer to her questions. She was delighted when one of the gentlemen in the party began to chat with Lady Michaels, thus removing any danger of that faux pas for the moment. But she knew her great-aunt would not forget, and like a bird with a stubborn worm, would continue to pull and pry.

Diana accepted Lord Cole's invitation to stroll about the gardens, and so she missed the duke's start when he realized she was missing. Rapidly searching the opposite booth, he saw Lord Cole had also disappeared, and his mouth tightened. Rising with alacrity, he suggested Cornelia might enjoy a stroll, but that lady had no intention of wandering about the dimly lit paths alone with him and his disgusting passions, and she was quick to deny him.

"Go with you, William," Lady Emily said, coming to the rescue. As the duke turned to escort her, he noticed Lady Michaels was staring at him again. She had been doing it all evening, even bending forward so as not to miss anything, and he wondered at it. Suddenly he saw her smile and nod, and he could have sworn she winked as well. How very strange! Was the old lady an eccentric?

Outside the booth, he took his sister's arm, then stood undecided for a moment.

"Went that way," Lady Emily told him, patting his arm with her free hand and striding off beside him.

"Dearest Em, you never miss a trick, do you?" Clare asked, his smile for her a little strained.

"Not often. It's the only amusement I get these days. But William—why this interest in Miss Travis still? Surely can't matter to you if she goes off with Dickie Cole. Believe he's harmless anyway, from what I've heard."

"What you're trying to say, dear sister, is that she should be of no concern to me anymore. I know that. And yet I cannot seem to forget her." They walked on in silence while Lady Emily swallowed all the questions that came to her lips, for why had her brother offered for Lady C. if he were still in love with Diana?

"Besides," he added, his voice even harsher than normal, "she shouldn't be jauntering about with another man when she's engaged to Maitland. And where *is* he? I've a mind to write to him and tell him he'd better get up to town while he still has a fiancée!"

"None of your business, William. Besides, this course you're pursuing can only lead to unhappiness. Beg you, forget Miss Travis. You've made your choice."

Just then they came face to face with the lady under discussion and her escort, returning from their stroll. The gentlemen bowed, the ladies curtsied, but when Lady Emily would have stopped to chat with Diana, she found the duke excusing them and hurrying her away. She promised herself she would call on Miss Travis soon, for there was some mystery here.

Fortunately for the duke's peace of mind, Roger Maitland arrived in town two days later. Not many more days after that, in Gentleman Jackson's Saloon, he had a chance to observe him sparring with the great man himself. The duke noticed that Roger stripped to advantage, and that although he was not in his weight class, had a lithe, athletic physique and a lightning jab. Clare leaned against the wall, determined to speak to him when his lesson should be over.

As he waited, his temper grew more and more explosive. How dare the man treat Diana so carelessly? Didn't he revere the prize he had won? And to wander up to town in his own good time, and never even write telling her his plans, to say nothing of being so nonchalant he didn't even mind his bride-to-be was making a spectacle of herself, raking about with all the young Corinthians, made his blood boil.

Accordingly, when Roger came over to him, wiping his face with a towel and smiling, Clare's expression turned even blacker. He was wishing he had the right to demand satisfaction and the names of Maitland's seconds.

"Well met, Your Grace," a mystified Roger said in greeting.

"I should say so indeed, sir," the duke retorted. "I cannot tell you how delightful it is to see you in London at last. I almost wrote to warn you you had better make haste or you would be sorry for the delay. But perhaps you do not care?"

Roger's brow furrowed in confusion. "Not care? About what? And why should I have made haste?"

"I think you know very well, and it is not for me to tell tales when you will find out soon enough for yourself," the duke snarled. Then he left the saloon abruptly, for he felt he could not remain talking to the man and keep his temper at the same time. As he strode down St. James Street on his way to his club, he wondered again why Diana had consented to marry a man who didn't seem to care a ha'penny for either her love or her reputation. In his eyes, Roger Maitland was a cad and a bounder, and he wished he could teach him a lesson he'd never forget!

That evening at Lady Markham's ball, he was furious to find Diana accompanied only by her elderly relative still.

Lady Michaels wondered what on earth the duke was looking so angry about now as she strove to keep him and Cornelia in view. She was glad Diana looked so very lovely in her new gown of rose muslin with its low round neck and tiny sleeves, and that the new length of it showed off to great advantage her well-turned ankles and slender feet in their ribboned sandals.

Several of the gentlemen seemed to agree with her, for Diana was never without a partner. Lady Michaels had to chuckle and poke Polly when she saw the Duke of Clare was also one of her admirers, for he was busy maneuvering Lady Cornelia so he might keep the girl in rose constantly under his eye.

The evening was very warm for spring, and some time after the supper dance, several of the guests went out to stroll up and down the terrace that adjoined the ballroom, to admire the new sliver of moon and enjoy the soft, welcome breeze. Lady Michaels saw Diana going out as well on Lord Evans's arm, and she began to count out loud.

"Eleven, twelve, thirteen—there he goes, dragging the beauteous Cornelia with him," she crowed to her companion. "I wondered how long it would take him to follow Di. What fun, Polly! *Now* do you agree there'll be fireworks?" She rose from her chair. "No, you stay here I want to see this for myself."

Threading her way around the dancing couples, Lady Michaels reached the terrace. There were a few people in sight, but none of them were the two pair she sought, so she went down the steps to the gravel path that led into the garden. She had not gone very far when she came upon the duke and his fianceé standing apart in the middle of the path, apparently deep in an argument.

To say Cornelia was delighted to see Lady Michaels was an understatement.

"My dear ma'am," she said, coming at once to her side, "how delightful to see you this evening! Have you come out for a breath of air? You must allow the duke and me to escort you for it is very dark here, is it not, and you must not take the risk of falling."

As she took Lady Michaels's arm, she added, "Clare! Offer the lady your support."

The duke extended his arm and the three of them continued through the garden, Lady Michaels a tiny, bobbing figure between her taller escorts. While Cornelia chatted lightly of the season, she felt somewhat stunned at being cast in the role of gooseberry, and she stole a look at the duke to see how he liked this new development. But he did not seem to notice for his eyes were searching each crossing of the path, his head turning this way and that until Lady Michaels decided to take pity on him. When Lady Cornelia stopped for a moment to retie her sandal, she whispered, "Not here! Gone in!" Then she winked.

The duke, who had not been attending, asked politely, "I beg your pardon, ma'am?" He was not sure he had really heard what she had said, but at that moment Cornelia rejoined them and their private conversation was over. When they reached the terrace again and she thanked him for his assistance, Clare was startled to see her wink at him again. But perhaps the poor old dear is afflicted with a tic, he thought. Perhaps it is only my imagination she is behaving so strangely. In any case, he told himself, she is no fit chaperone for Diana. Why, just look what had happened already this evening, Diana roaming about in the dark with Pierpont Evans who, although he was a very good friend, was not noted for either good sense or strong self-control.

Lady Michaels rejoined her wide-eyed companion and told her everything in a loud stage whisper. In conclusion she said, "I wish I knew why La Cornelia was so very friendly. She clutched my arm like a lifeline! I'm sure she should have been wishing me at the devil for interrupting such a golden opportunity, alone in the dark with her fiancé. Don't you agree the modern generation doesn't seem to have any idea how to go on, Polly? Now if it had been me, I'd have had my arms around him in a thrice, and done a great deal more besides!"

Lady Michaels chortled so at her own wit, she finally had to be helped to the lady's withdrawing room to recover.

As was their custom now, she and her great-niece retired to the library after the ball to compare notes, and she retold the story with glee. Diana tried to look suitably impressed, but she didn't see that Clare following her into the garden was anywhere near the sign of progress her great-aunt did. She could not help feeling discouraged, for the season went on and on and the duke's engagement showed no signs of being broken by either party. Sometimes, when she would look up at a large gathering to find the duke's eyes on her face, she would have a wild surge of hope that perhaps things would work out after all, and she would go home to dream of it. Tossing and turning in bed, she would make plans and invent situations where she would find herself alone with Clare. Miraculously he would declare he could not live without her, no matter how society disapproved. In this way she lived vicariously through carriage accidents where the duke swept her up in his arms to make sure she wasn't hurt, blazing conflagrations where he saved her just before the building collapsed, boating accidents where she almost drowned, and fevers where she would have died if he had not nursed her back to health himself.

One night after she had finally fallen asleep, she even dreamt that Sir Percy, Dickie Cole, and Pierpont Evans had kidnapped her. They were taking her away in a balloon, only to be foiled by the duke at the very last moment. He replaced her in the basket with Cornelia, who floated upward with her three escorts, waving good-bye with her diamond-bedecked hand as the duke and Diana melted into each other's arms.

When none of these marvelous things happened in daylight, she was left in the same predicament as before—without him and without any possibility of attaching him. She found it very depressing and it was all she could do to keep her flagging spirits up.

Roger Maitland came to call and was presented to Lady Michaels, who was delighted to meet him and made much of him during his visit. But when he asked them to honor him with their company on a drive in the park the following afternoon, the old lady denied him.

"So kind of you, Mr. Maitland," she said, "but unfortunately I'm engaged tomorrow. Why don't you and Di go without me? I'm sure you'll take the greatest care of her. And since you are so new-come to town, we would be pleased to have you join my party for dinner and the theater on Friday next."

So a time was set for the drive, and the evening party accepted before Roger bowed himself out. As soon as the door closed behind him, Diana turned to her great-aunt. "What a whisker, ma'am! 'Engaged,' indeed! And *what* dinner and theater party? You're up to something. Tell me!"

Lady Michaels smiled. "You didn't tell me he was so handsome, child. That fresh color, his open expression—that outstanding build. I can see why the duke is concerned about him, my, yes! We'll make good use of Mr. Maitland. Perhaps he's even the weapon we've been searching for. I never did think Nottingham, Evans, or Cole would turn the trick. Now, you're to wear the new scarlet driving dress and that bewitching new hat, and you will be very, very charming to Mr. Maitland."

Diana had to smile. "But wouldn't that be too obvious, ma'am? Of course I'm fond of Roger, and it won't be at all difficult to be charming to him, but I fail to see how that will change anything."

"Trust me, dear Di," Lady Michaels said before she almost skipped from the room in her excitement.

And so all London society was treated to the sight of Roger Maitland and Miss Diana Travis not only driving together in the park the following afternoon, but conversing with laughter and animation as well. The duke had the good fortune to observe them himself, for he was riding with Lady Cornelia and his mother in the dowager's black landau.

"Look there," she said, pointing with her parasol. "Isn't that Miss . . . Miss? and her fiancé, Mr. Maitland?"

Cornelia stole a glance at Clare. His face was set in rigid planes and his jaw jutted aggressively. She hurried into speech.

"You see, Clare, it is just as I told you. And now that

Roger has arrived in town to see to her, there is no need for you, er, *us,* to worry about Diana anymore."

The dowager wished she wouldn't speak so sharply to dear William, as Cornelia added, "I've never seen her looking so well. But then, they do say love puts a bloom on women, don't they? How happy we must all be for her."

The duke nodded curtly, and tipped his hat as the two carriages passed each other. He had seen Diana put her hand on Roger's arm and the warm smile she gave him as she did so, and he felt a certain bleak satisfaction that warred with the pangs of disappointment in his breast.

From that time on he seemed to see the two of them wherever he went, for Lady Michaels was very busy promoting this new scheme of hers. Unfortunately, it just reinforced the duke's belief in their engagement, and instead of making him mad with jealousy and forcing him to take action as Lady Michaels had hoped, it only made him realize he must accept the situation in spite of his extreme reluctance to do so.

But one evening at a gala ball, the duke was surprised to find Diana dancing and flirting with all her old beaux, much as she had done before Maitland came to town. He frowned. What was this all about, he wondered, and why did Maitland allow it? He watched the two of them closely, and although Maitland danced with her twice, he made no push to remain by her side or take her in to supper. Sir Percy Nottingham did that while Maitland joined another group with every appearance of enjoyment. He did not even take a seat that would allow him to keep Diana under his eye, but sat with his back to her and never turned even once to see what she was about. Clare fumed.

After supper, he found himself standing near Maitland.

He was not dancing, rather he was discussing the latest race with some friends. Meanwhile, his betrothed romped through a lively schottische with Lord Evans.

The duke strode up to the group. "A word with you, Maitland," he said so abruptly the other men took their leave at once.

"Your Grace," Roger said easily, wondering what was amiss with the man now, but determined to be pleasant. "A delightful evening, is it not? I'm always struck by the gaiety and beauty of the London scene when I've not been here for some time."

Clare did not bother to reply to this pleasantry. "Look there, man," he said, indicating Diana with an inclination of his head. Roger thought it best to do as he was bid. Diana was now dancing with Sir Percy, and as the two men stood watching her, she put back her head and laughed at something the young man was saying. Clare saw Sir Percy bend his head close so he might whisper in her ear, and it was hard to contain his wrath as he turned back to Maitland.

"Well?" he demanded.

"Miss Travis, you mean, sir?" Roger asked, finding himself in uncharted waters once again. "She is looking very lovely tonight. And she appears to be enjoying her first season tremendously. I'm delighted for her."

"I wonder you can be so nonchalant, Mr. Maitland," the duke replied, keeping a tight rein on his temper. "I find your permissiveness incomprehensible, and more than a little sickening. If Miss Travis were *my* betrothed, I'd never let her carry on in such a way, nor permit other men to hang about her so."

"Nor would I," Roger said coolly. "*If* she were my betrothed, which alas, she is not. I especially dislike Sir Per—"

"Do you mean to tell me you aren't engaged to Diana?" the duke interrupted, grasping his arm in his confusion.

Roger glanced down at the crushed sleeve of his evening coat and then up to the duke's face. He was sure he had never seen such agony on anyone's face before, and he wondered at it. Flushing, Clare removed that iron hand.

"But I had it on good authority that you were engaged to be married," he exclaimed. Roger noticed his eyes narrowing, saw the way he was clenching his fists. Although he was no coward, he could still feel the pressure of the duke's strong grip, and he was glad he wasn't to be the recipient of the man's rage. He hastened to explain, obscurely sorry for the misery that came over the duke's face as he spoke.

"I asked her to marry me before I left Stafford Hall," he concluded. "She told me, however, she could never love me that way. It was a grievous disappointment to me, but I have not completely abandoned hope, sir."

"I suggest you abandon it now, Mr. Maitland!" Clare said harshly before he strode away without another word.

10

Although the duke's first impulse was to rush across the room and confront Cornelia with what he had learned, only a moment's reflection reminded him this would not do. A crowded ballroom was hardly the place for the kind of conversation he envisioned having with the woman, and they couldn't leave so early without causing all kinds of speculation and gossip. He forced himself to wait out the remainder of the evening, somewhat detached from the merriment around him, by thinking of how he would handle the situation. Even in his anger he felt a lightening in his heart that Diana was free and didn't love Roger Maitland after all. He wished he might speak to her, but until he had Cornelia's explanation for her part in the deception, he dared not approach her.

For her part, Cornelia was enjoying the evening immensely. She had been introduced to an army captain recently returned from duty abroad, and he was so obvious in his admiration for the most beautiful woman he had ever seen, so fervent in his compliments, and so attentive and worshipful, that she did not even notice Clare's brooding expression and set face. When at last he came to escort her home, it was to find the gallant captain bowing low over her hand, and Lady Cornelia blushing in delight.

As the duke helped her into his town carriage, Cornelia finally noticed his black expression. Feeling that perhaps she had angered him by neglecting him all evening, she was careful to chat lightly during the drive home.

At the door, she steeled herself for their ritual good-night kiss, but Clare grasped her arm and sounded the knocker instead.

"I'd like a word with you, Cornelia," he explained. She wanted to deny him, but he gave her no time to refuse, telling the butler when he opened the door that he wished to be private with Lady Cornelia and they were on no account to be disturbed. Then he marched the lady across the hall to the drawing room and shut the doors firmly behind them.

"My dear Clare," Cornelia said as she removed her stole and took a seat some distance away from him. She was more than a little alarmed now. "Won't it wait till morning? I'm so very tired, and it is so late. Besides, I don't think it proper for us to be alone at this hour even though we are engaged. 'Do not wish to be disturbed,' indeed! Fine doings for the Duke of Clare! I'm sure the butler is thinking the most dreadful things!"

She tried to laugh, but that laugh caught in her throat when she saw the duke's unchanged expression. He had gone to stand by the dying fire, but he never took his eyes from her face.

"Now you will have the goodness to explain to me, Cornelia, how you came to tell me Diana Travis was engaged to Roger Maitland, when it is no such thing," he said in a quiet voice that was all the more disturbing for its very control.

Cornelia had been expecting this for some time. In

fact, she knew Maitland's prolonged absence from town had been the only thing that had allowed her to keep her deception so long. Still, she was a good actress, and her pretense of startled surprise would have fooled anyone.

"They are *not* engaged?" she gasped. "Are you sure?"

"I heard the truth from Mr. Maitland himself this very evening."

"Perhaps the engagement was broken when Roger saw how she had been behaving during his absence. You remarked it yourself, Clare. So forward—so flirtatious! Yes, that must be it! Roger must have felt he had no choice but to terminate the engagement. I do feel for him, poor man."

Clare shook his head, his hazel eyes still intent on her face.

"They were never engaged at all. Never. And yet you were the one who told me they were. What mischief-making was this, Cornelia? Why did you lie to me?" He paused as she took her handkerchief from her reticule and buried her face in it. "Come, I'm waiting to hear your explanation," he continued. "You've been very busy about Diana's affairs, haven't you? Will you force me to guess the reason?"

Cornelia came to him and raised sad eyes to his face. "How can you accuse me of being so deceitful, my dear? I can't tell you how your mistrust hurts me. Naturally I thought they were engaged, for I overheard Diana discussing Roger's proposal with her sister. Anne told her what an advantageous match it would be, and I heard Diana agreeing with her. What else was I supposed to think?"

She pretended to cry, all the while watching him as he turned away to pace the room, and she added in a rueful tone, "I am sure I beg your pardon, and I will beg hers, too, if you insist on it, but the implication was clear and I was sure the engagement was a foregone conclusion. But my dear, I fail to see why it is so upsetting to you. What can it matter if little Diana Travis is engaged or not? It has nothing to do with us."

She went to him and for the first time voluntarily put her arms around him. The duke, in one firm, calm motion, set her aside. For a moment he stared down at her and Cornelia was suddenly afraid of what he might do, or say. His eyes were so angry, so shadowed, that she hurried into speech again.

"Come, my dear Clare! You are behaving so strangely! And if Diana is not engaged yet, you may be sure she will be before long. Just consider all her admirers. It is kind of you to trouble yourself about her, but Lady Michaels has her well in hand. And after all, it is our engagement that is important."

The duke walked away from her to the door where he turned to face her again. "I intend to call on you tomorrow afternoon, ma'am, after I have had a chance to decide what to do. I trust you will be sure to be here, and to arrange for our interview to be completely private."

Cornelia put out her hand, but before she could speak again, he was gone. She sank down in a chair. She was very worried. Clare had not even pretended to believe her, nor had he smiled, or kissed her good-night. She stayed in the drawing room for some time, and when she went up to bed at last, she had formulated a plan of action.

She had heard Clare and Lady Emily that same afternoon, discussing a ride they were planning to take to Richmond and so she was not afraid she would meet him when she presented her card at Clare House several hours later and asked to see the dowager.

Her Grace kept her waiting half an hour before she allowed her to come to her boudoir. The lady was a little miffed with her dear Cornelia who had been nowhere near as attentive since she had become engaged. She had even spoken sharply to the dowager when she had been enumerating her latest aches and pains. Gone were the smiles and gentle concern. Now she was often impatient and cold.

Cornelia smiled as she bent to kiss the cool cheek that was raised to her before she took a chair nearby.

"And to what do I owe this unexpected visit, Cornelia? Not that I'm not delighted to see you. Finally."

Cornelia recognized her error, and hastened to make amends.

"My dear ma'am! My apologies for my neglect when I have been longing to see you, but I knew you were not feeling well and I could not bear to burden or alarm you with my little problems." She took out her handkerchief as she spoke, and wiped her dry eyes.

The dowager sat up a little straighter. "What problems? Come, you may tell me. It is not Clare, I hope, who is distressing you?"

Cornelia nodded and pretended to sob. "I fear he is about to cry off, ma'am. Oh, I cannot bear it! Me, the daughter of an earl, jilted! The humiliation of it—the scandal—the gossip. I shall never live it down!"

The dowager took a restoring sniff of her salts before she clutched them tightly to her chest. Something told her she was sure to need them again. "What nonsense is this? Clare would never be so outré unless there was an excellent reason. What has been happening between you?" she demanded.

"It is Diana Travis, ma'am. She has been throwing herself at Clare and I fear it has turned his head. You must understand it is not in my nature to be as . . . as abandoned as she is. I would never, *could* never stoop to such earthy behavior."

The dowager did not think to question her for particulars for she was extremely shocked. "Certainly not! It is not to be thought of," she exclaimed, and emboldened by this support, Cornelia continued, "In fact, dear ma'am, I fear she has bewitched him for when he discovered last evening Diana was not engaged to Mr. Maitland after all, he accused me of lying to him about it."

She sniffed and the dowager was so moved, she rose from her chaise to go and pat her on the shoulder.

"Never say so, Cornelia. I am sure you must be mistaken. But if you remember, I told you the engagement you planned was of too long a duration. Why you insisted on waiting until Christmas to marry dear Clare, I'll never know. Men are so . . . so impatient!"

Cornelia stared up at her and there was no need to playact now.

"But I cannot bear it," she whispered. "I . . . I have the greatest dislike for . . . for anything of that nature."

The dowager nodded and tottered back to her chaise. "Say no more. I understand completely. You are just as I was, all sensitivity. But if you would be Duchess of Clare, you must put up with it, distasteful as it is." She looked away, two red spots flaming on her sunken cheeks. "I suggest you insist on the marriage taking place as soon as you can contrive it. When Clare has you to wife he will not think of Miss . . . Miss? again. And you will be brave and accept that part of marriage, no matter how repugnant it is to any woman of delicacy and refinement."

Her voice died away, but then she straightened up. "Try not to dwell on it, my dear. I daresay you will become accustomed, and after my son has his heir, perhaps some other arrangement can be made. But what a shame you are so strong!"

Cornelia stared at her bewildered, but the dowager would not look at her as she continued, "I mean, since you are in the best of health, there can be no excuse. In matters of that nature, a weak heart is such a comfort! But do not fear Clare will cry off. You may rely on me."

She did not explain what she had in mind to do, but Cornelia was feeling much better when she took her leave. At least the dowager was firmly on her side again.

At that moment in Richmond, the duke and Lady Emily were strolling beside the river, trailing their horses behind them. Lady Emily could see her brother was troubled about something but before she could ask he told her everything he had learned the previous evening, and Cornelia's reply when he had taxed her with it.

"But what good does it do me to know whether or not she lied to me?" he concluded. "Even if Diana isn't engaged, *I* am. And you know, Em, there is no way I can break it off if Cornelia is determined to marry me."

Lady Emily nodded grimly. "Told you the Lady C. had ways to snare you, William. Would say you're most definitely trapped by her now. But let me think . . . perhaps there is some way . . ."

Since nothing immediately leapt to mind, her voice died away. The duke put an arm around her shoulder and gave her an affectionate squeeze.

"Dearest Em, if you can show me a way to escape the lady's coils, you'll have my undying gratitude and I'll find our mother a companion to replace you at once."

His sister laughed. "With an incentive like that, m'dear, shall put my mind to work on the problem posthaste. Would suggest you stay away from Lady C. in the meantime. You're so angry, you're sure to upset the applecart! Get out of London for a while instead. You can't see Miss Travis in any case until Lady C. has been vanquished."

Feeling somewhat better for laying his problems on his sister's broad shoulders, the duke agreed to her plan and escorted her back to Clare House.

While he wrote a cold note to Lady Cornelia canceling their meeting for that afternoon and telling her he had been called out of town for an indefinite period, Lady Emily changed her habit for a morning gown and took a hackney to Lady Michaels's town house. No sense puttin' it off, she told herself as she gave her card to the lady's butler. Shall speak to Miss Travis myself and find out her feelin' for Clare.

But she was to be disappointed for Diana had gone out to Hocker's Library to return a book for her great-aunt, and had not yet returned. She would have gone away except Lady Michaels came into the hall and recognized her at once.

"You must allow me the pleasure of entertaining you, m'lady, in my great-niece's absence," she said after she had introduced herself. "How disappointed Di will be she was not here. But perhaps there is something I can do to assist you?"

She ushered Lady Emily into the library, instructed her butler to bring them both a glass of sherry, and then insisted her visitor sit down and tell her in what way she could be of service.

Lady Emily hesitated briefly. But as she stared at the old lady, she saw her warm expression and such a twinkle of understanding in her eyes that she was reassured, and taking a deep breath, she plunged into her story.

"Don't know if you are aware of it, ma'am, but

m'brother—Clare, that is—has just discovered that Miss Travis is not engaged to Mr. Maitland as he had been led to believe."

"Di engaged? To Maitland? She's never been engaged to him!" Lady Michaels said, much stunned.

"Well, William was told she became engaged in Cuckfield, and when she did not respond to his letter, he was sure of it."

Lady Michaels began to bounce up and down in her chair, a sure sign she was excited.

"Shall we finish this bout with the gloves off, m'lady?" she asked. "I think if we pool our knowledge we might be able to shed more light on this puzzling situation. So *that* was why he said what he did to her in Almacks!"

Emily begged to know what he had said, and the two ladies sat together for over an hour. Their conversation was interspersed with many a "can it be true?" and "I don't believe it!" and "say you so indeed?" and when the tale was completely told, Lady Michaels put down her wineglass with a snap and said with loathing, "Cornelia!"

Her guest nodded. "Definitely agree with you, ma'am. Cornelia indeed. This is all her doin' for she's been tryin' to trap my brother this age, aided by m'mother. But now they are engaged, don't see any way William can escape her. He can't ask for his release when she's claimed it was all a mistake and begged his pardon. As for his letter, all she has to do is deny she ever saw it at all."

Lady Michaels nodded glumly. "I am afraid nothing occurs to me as a solution, Lady Emily. And yet there must be something . . ."

Lady Emily rose. "Shall call on you again, ma'am, if I may. Can assume then Miss Travis does care for William?" She paused until Lady Michaels nodded emphatically. "So relieved to hear it! I've sent m'brother out of town. He's no use in this matter, and we can't have him murderin' Lady C. in a fit of rage. Give my best to Miss Travis—if you are goin' to tell her what we discovered, that is."

Lady Michaels frowned. "Terrible temper, my niece," she confided. "I don't like to think what she might do. She and Clare are well matched there. On the other hand, she's been so unhappy for so long. I must think on it."

The two ladies parted in the greatest amiability, and Lady Michaels was still pondering when Diana returned from her errand and came to join her in the library.

It was not long before Diana had the whole story, for Lady Michaels could not bear to keep her in suspense. Her heart gave a great leap when she heard that Clare had only proposed to Lady Cornelia because he thought her promised to another, and lost to him forever. Then her ecstatic smile faded.

"But what good does knowing it do? He is still tied to that . . . that . . ."

"Exactly, dear Di. It's not necessary to say what you had in mind to say, for I know what it is. But something is sure to happen. I can't imagine the Duke of Clare allowing himself to be dragged unprotesting into marriage with a woman of that stamp, for 'lady' I can call her no longer. We must do nothing. We must wait and see."

And so in the following days, nothing is exactly what they did. Diana went to parties and teas, attended the theater and a concert. She did not see the duke for he had taken his sister's advice and retired to the country, and she saw Lady Cornelia only rarely and that at a distance, which was just as well for the lady's smooth cheeks and red-gold curls.

Cornelia was in a quandary. After waiting in some trepidation for the duke to call, she had received only hi cold note, and there had been no further word from him. She hurried to tell the dowager, who nodded and immediately set about the plan she had conceived. Her Grace became very social, going about in company more than was her general custom, and making sure the rumors she was spreading about Diana Travis fell on fertile ears.

"I should not mention it, of course," she whispered to a Mrs. Hawley who bore the palm as London's most accomplished gossip, "but I have heard . . ." The dowager closed her eyes for a moment in disgust as Mrs. Hawley edged closer in her chair, her little black eyes eager, "I have heard that Miss . . . Miss? Miss *Travis* is no better than she should be."

"You don't say," the other lady breathed.

"It is not generally known but she is, oh, dear—depraved. I wonder any decent man can be found to marry her after her behavior this season. She was caught in a compromising situation with a gentleman whose identity, out of delicacy to his family's position, I cannot reveal."

"She was? I wonder I did not hear of it earlier . . . ?"

"It is still not generally known, thanks to Lady Michaels's influence. And I have it on good authority, although I blush to relate it, that once she even spent the night in a gentleman's hunting box, sans chaperone, of course. She is man-mad. How my heart goes out to her poor parents!"

Mrs. Hawley nodded as the dowager concluded, "But not a word of this! I wonder Emma Michaels continues to house her. If it were up to me, I'd send her back to the country and pay someone handsomely to marry her before her dissipations become known."

Mrs. Hawley extolled Lady Michaels's nobleness and promised not to breathe a word, and the dowager excused herself to speak to Mrs. Boothe and Lady Felton-Moore.

In a very short space of time, the talk was all over town, for Mrs. Hawley told two of her particular bosom bows, who told two of theirs, although in the strictest confidence, of course. Lady Michaels might have scotched the rumors in short order, but her rheumatism was acting up and she was forced to retire to her bed while the gossip spread unchecked.

Diana was soon aware there was something wrong. She saw the looks and heard the whispers, although she had no idea what they meant. Nor could she discover what she might have done to make some of the highest sticklers cut her. The Follett brothers, on orders from their mother, were the first of her beaux to decamp, and they were followed in short order by Lord Cole.

Only Lord Evans and Sir Percy Nottingham continued faithful, and for them she was grateful. She thought to ask them if they had any idea what the matter was, but she did not feel she knew them well enough to broach the subject. Besides, Sir Percy was becoming very strange in his manner, almost unpleasantly familiar in a way she could not like. If only Roger Maitland had not gone out of town to a race meeting with friends, she thought. I know I could ask him.

With her great-aunt in such pain, Diana did not like to bother her with this new, peculiar turn of events, but when she would have retired from society, Lady Michaels would not allow her to do so.

"I know you'd prefer to sit home dreaming of William Rawlings, dear Di, but it won't do. As long as Cornelia continues to sally about flaunting her betrothal, you'll make an effort to remain very much in view. Drat this rheumatism!" She shifted her aching bones, and Diana kissed her and promised she would do as she was told.

She had agreed to a drive with Sir Percy one afternoon

although she wished she might have refused him. But what possible harm can come to me in Hyde Park? she thought, trying to smile at her escort. Sir Percy leered back. He was a veritable Pink of the Ton. Although he wasn't very tall, he was always dressed in the first stare, and he was full of airs and graces for he considered himself quite the top-of-the-trees man, and a devil with the ladies.

When he had heard the rumors about Diana, he had been stunned by his good fortune, but in the days that followed the lady did not seem inclined to follow his lead. Indeed, his most flagrant hints were met only with an astonished stare or a rather frigid reply. He decided Diana was being coy; that what she really wanted him to do was sweep her off her feet before she succumbed to his masculine charms.

Being agreeable to such a romantic notion, Sir Percy made arrangements to sweep.

Diana was quick to notice he was not heading in the direction of the park, but when she asked where they were going, Sir Percy only smiled and told her he had a surprise for her.

She would have liked to refuse the treat and beg to be set down, but she told herself she was being unduly alarmed. Surely there was no harm in Sir Percy. He was such a fop. Accordingly, she settled back as he wove his team through the busy London streets, making light conversation all the while. She did not really become alarmed until they reached the outskirts of town and he sprung the team.

Bowling along a country road at a fast clip that had her clutching her smart driving hat, Diana demanded to know where they were going.

"I did not think you meant to travel out of town, sir," she said as coldly as she could.

"Not far, dearest Diana, not far! You must not be impatient," Sir Percy told her, wishing he did not need to keep both hands on the reins.

"I beg your pardon?" she said, stiffening at this overly familiar form of address.

Sir Percy giggled. "Dearest, *darling* Diana! I'm kidnapping you, my poppet. Isn't it exciting?"

Diana swallowed. She could not leap from the curricle for at the pace they were traveling she was sure to be killed. She grasped the side of the seat with one hand and resolved to box the young man's ears for such impertinence. Just as soon as he halted the team, that is.

Sir Percy turned into a dusty lane that ended in the yard of a small cottage. A boy came running to hold the horses, and Sir Percy sprang from his seat before Diana could make good her threat. She could see a fat woman wiping her hands on her apron in the doorway of the cottage, and a farmhand gawking at her from a nearby field, and rather than make a scene in public, she permitted Sir Percy to help her from the curricle.

He pressed her hand and she withdrew it from his clasp in haste. "Hopefully there is some plausible explanation for your unusual behavior, sir?" she asked, her voice dripping icicles.

"Come inside, Diana," he urged. "I can't explain with such a crowd staring at us. Lord, they must think us some kind of raree show! But yokels, y'know . . ."

As he spoke he hustled her to the door of the cottage. The fat woman curtsied and indicated the front parlor, smirking all the while. Sir Percy shut the door firmly on her avid face.

"*Now,* my dear Diana," he said, stripping off his gloves

and coming to take her in his arms. Diana took a great deal of satisfaction in boxing his ears as hard as she could before she backed away from him, saying, "Idiot! Whatever gave you the idea I would welcome your attentions? I've never been so insulted in my life!"

Staggering a little, Sir Percy tried to smile through his watering eyes, and ignoring the ringing in his ears, he said, "Now, now, little love! Such shyness and reluctance are most inappropriate, for we both know what you are like, don't we? And at long last we are completely alone as I'm sure we've both wished to be. Come!"

Diana could see the boy who had taken charge of the team peering in at the window, and she could hear the fat woman's asthmatic breathing at the keyhole, so she could hardly agree they were alone. But this was dangerous ground and she did not point it out to him.

He drew near and tried to take her in his arms again, and she kicked him in the shin. He howled and hopped backward to massage his aching leg. Diana noticed the boy at the window had been joined by the farmhand, and it gave her courage to say, "I do not know where you got the idea I should like such disgusting familiarities. I think you have gone mad! Take me home!"

Sir Percy held out his hands in supplication, but having been stung twice, he did not try to approach her again. The lady seemed to be very angry, and he knew she could be dangerous, and he would be the first to admit he was not especially brave.

"Now, my dear, such playacting," he said in a light, funning voice. "Come sit down and we'll discuss this over a cup of tea—"

"No, thank you. If you don't take me home at once, I'll scream," Diana said. Sir Percy eyed the two fists she had made in trepidation.

"But there is no need for this maidenly reserve and defense of your flown virtue, m'dear. All London knows what you are like. Assure you, all over town."

"What is all over town?" Diana demanded, coming to stand before him.

He retreated behind a chair. "Why, that you spent a night with Tommy Neston, of course. And then there was your adventure with Lord Slayton on the post road to Bath, and—"

"I will kill you for those lies!" Diana exclaimed as she picked up a pewter plate from the mantel and threatened him with it.

"Ssshh," Sir Percy warned, finger to his lips. "I only hired this cottage for the afternoon and there mustn't be any dustups. I promised the good wife her furniture would be safe."

"Did you indeed, you horrible little worm?" Diana retorted. "Well, it was all for naught. I'll have you know you've been misled in my character, for I've never done any of those terrible things you mentioned!"

Sir Percy decided to try one more time. "But my adorable one, it is completely safe! My heart is at your feet. You needn't fear I'll love and tell."

He rushed to her and pulled her into his arms for a kiss. It was not a very successful embrace, for Diana was pummeling his back with the plate, and swinging her head back and forth to escape his seeking lips. Finally the top of her head caught him smartly across the bridge of his nose.

"Oww!" he bellowed, clutching his bleeding nose as he staggered away. Diana went to the door and flung it open. The fat woman, a slatternly looking girl, and two cats almost fell into the room at her feet.

"We do not stay," she announced in her grandest, most

haughty manner. "Have m'lord's curricle brought 'round at once."

She marched past her astonished audience to stand waiting in the doorway, her arms crossed and one foot tapping furiously. The farmhand tugged his forelock and hurried to do her bidding, and Sir Percy soon appeared behind her, clutching a napkin to his nose.

"Humble apologies, Miss Travis," he muttered thickly through the cloth. "Terrible mistake. Must beg your pardon."

"Oh, do be quiet, you stupid man!" Diana snapped, moving ahead of him into the yard in her impatience to be gone.

When the curricle arrived, she climbed up to the driver's seat. Sir Percy would have protested until he realized how impossible it would be for him to tool the team when it was still necessary for him to hold the bloodied napkin to his nose.

Not a word was exchanged on the ride back. As soon as Diana reached the more fashionable part of town, she halted the team and climbed down.

"I shall take a hackney from here, sir," she announced. "And I do sincerely hope I never, ever, have to see your face again."

As she marched away, Sir Percy picked up the reins and drove off, both bloody and bowed and most thoroughly routed. How he had been so misled in the lady's character he did not know, but he hoped that when Miss Travis calmed down she would not feel she had to mention the excursion. If she did, he'd be forced to rusticate for a considerable period until people stopped discussing his being guilty of such bad ton.

Diana did mention it, but only to two people. When she reached home, she discovered Lady Emily come to call, and as soon as they were alone, poured out the whole tale. Lady Emily was appalled although she could not help laughing a little at Diana's description of how she had saved herself. While they were still discussing it, Lord Evans was announced. Diana would have waited until she could be private with Lady Emily again before continuing, but she was overruled.

"Pierpont is the man we want," Lady Emily said firmly. "Can be trusted. Good friend of William's. Besides, knows everyone in town."

Lord Evans tried to look suitably pleased by the compliment as he assured Diana he would do anything he could to help her.

"But who can be spreading such terrible gossip about me?" Diana asked after she had told her story again. She sounded so bewildered, Lady Emily patted her hand. "Cornelia? But why would she do such a thing? For spite?"

Lady Emily frowned. "Doesn't make sense. She'd never dare lest William find out. Been most circumspect, has Lady C. these past few days."

After being pledged to secrecy, Lord Evans was put in the picture as regards Lady Cornelia. He was a little disappointed to discover Miss Travis was as good as promised to his friend the duke. Somehow it seemed most unfair that one man had managed to capture not one, but two, of the season's brightest stars. Still, he managed to swallow his chagrin.

"Allow me to ask a few questions about town, m'lady, Miss Travis," he said as he was leaving. "I'll be most discreet, word of an Evans! And perhaps you might also inquire of your acquaintance, Lady Emily?"

After the two had gone, Diana was left to pace the drawing room. She was no longer in the white heat she had been during Sir Percy's advances, but she was still extremely angry. Her mother would have known how dangerous she could be in this condition, but Mrs. Travis was safely out of the way in Eastham, and there was no one to stem to flood of resentment and the sincere wish for revenge that festered in Diana's heart. Oh, yes, she told herself, she would exact payment for this, just see if she didn't!

Lady Emily made a few diffident inquiries that evening at a reception she attended, but since she only asked Lady Cates who was so deaf you might tell her the most dreadful stories and know they would be safe with her, and Mrs. Hendricks, so new-come to town she had not heard any of the latest on dits, her efforts were fruitless. Unfortunately, Emily Rawlings was not cut out for intrigue.

Lord Evans, on the other hand, went at once to his mother, laid the whole story before her, and prepared to take her advice. The next morning he escorted her on a call to Mrs. Hawley who professed horror that such slander should spread throughout the ton.

"My dear Lady Evans, I am much shocked," she proclaimed. "But when the Dowager Duchess of Clare told me the story, I did not like to question her even though I've always felt Miss Travis a most modest, lovely girl. I certainly did not repeat the story, you may be sure!" Here, Mrs. Hawley drew herself up, her bosom swelling with injured dignity. Lady Evans was quick to say she would never suspect her of such a thing.

From Mrs. Hawley's the two Evans drove to Lady Felton-Moore's, who, after much backing and filling, was finally induced to admit her informant had also been the dowager duchess. There was the usual ten minutes spent calming the lady as regards to any suspicion she might have spread the gossip. This time it was easier, Lord Evans having his lines down pat, and his face under perfect control.

As he helped his mother back into her carriage, he said, " 'Pon my word, Ma, why would the duke's *mother* spread such a tale? Both those ladies must have been mistaken, or else they're covering up for someone else."

Lady Evans shook her head. "My dear Pierpont, you must remember that 'hell hath no fury like a woman scorned.' "

Lord Evans looked askance, hoping his mother was not about to turn literary on him. "But that cock won't fight, Ma! Cornelia is the one who might end up being scorned. Not saying she will, mind, but . . ."

His mother smiled in a superior way. "But the dowager has thrown her support to Lady Cornelia, hasn't she? Therefore, if the duke wishes to break the engagement, he is scorning her choice."

"What devious, horrid minds women have," Lord Evans muttered. His mother chortled.

"Someday you'll find out for yourself how devious, my son. And I'll thank you not to call me 'Ma' in that detestable lower-class way!"

Lord Evans grinned at her. "Do we have enough proof? These morning calls on all the old tabbys are not my idea of amusement."

His mother prevailed on him to make one more, but neither of them was surprised when Miss Smythe said she had heard the rumor from Lady Felton-Moore, and her sister, Miss Harriet, said her informant had been Mrs. Hawley. Both elderly spinsters promised they would do all they could to repair the damage done to an innocent girl's reputation.

Lord Evans was delighted to escape at last, to take his

mother home and give her a warm hug and a kiss for her help.

He decided to see Diana alone. It would be too embarrassing for him to have to reveal to Lady Emily that it had been her own dear mother who had been the source of the malicious mischief. But perhaps Diana would know how to break the news to her? He told himself females were much better at that sort of thing as he set out for Lady Michaels's house.

11

The Duke of Clare, impatiently waiting at Clare Court in the interim, had decided to take matters into his own hands if he did not hear from his sister by the end of the week. It was extremely difficult for him as a man of action, to do nothing but wait to be called back to town after Lady Emily had prepared his way. For the first few days of his exile he had managed to keep busy by a diligent application to estate matters, but all too soon his interest lagged.

He did make a morning call to Stafford Hall and he enjoyed talking about Diana to her sister Anne. He told her how Diana's season was progressing and how popular she was. Anne listened carefully, and as soon as the duke took his leave, hurried to write a letter to her mother in which she was more than a little optimistic about Diana's future.

"I would tell you, dear Mother, that Clare appears to be fairly caught by Di, although this engagement of his to Cornelia is worrisome. However, by his manner I would think it on the verge of being dissolved for he did not mention her to me once. Finally I was forced—from politeness, you know—to inquire for her. I do wish you could have seen his face, so cold! And when he said she was well, it was couched in the curtest of terms."

Not knowing he was the subject of such intense interest, the duke returned to Clare Court to find the post had been delivered. Riffling through it, he saw he had received a letter from his sister at last, and one from Lady Michaels as well. This last was so unusual he felt a great reluctance to open it. Finally he gave orders that he was not to be disturbed for any reason and went into his library and shut the door. He was no coward, but he fortified himself with a glass of wine before he sat down to read.

He broke the seal of Emily's letter first. It was perhaps unfortunate that she had written to him so soon after learning the gossipmonger was none other than their own mother, for she was so filled with shame and remorse, she could not be calm. Diana, who no more than Pierpont Evans had been able to face telling her such dreadful news, had finally confessed everything to her great-aunt. Lady Michaels, free at last from the pain of her rheumatic attack, had volunteered her services as envoy, much to Diana's relief. Although the old lady tried to be as kind as possible, there was no way to soften the blow. Mortified, Lady Emily had rushed home to inform her brother, and Lady Michaels was moved to take quill in hand as well, hoping her communication might temper the duke's reaction to his sister's news.

William Rawlings swore and crumpled up his sister's letter before he threw it on the fire and rose to pace the library. How *dare* his mother do such an infamous thing? It was just as well she was not in residence at the Court, for spells or no spells, he would have given her a thundering scold! As for Sir Percy, he might count himself lucky to escape with no more than a horsewhipping, when the duke caught up with him.

After another glass of wine, Clare's temper had cooled

somewhat and he was able to think more coherently. Emily had not given any reason for the dowager's behavior, but it was not hard to make the connection. Cornelia was behind it in some way. Perhaps she had not instigated the plan, but she must have spoken to his mother, who had then decided to meddle, with the worst possible results. He decided grimly that the Lady Cornelia had a lot to answer for. It would give him no end of satisfaction to make sure she did.

Nodding grimly to himself, and taking a deep, fortifying breath, he opened Lady Michaels's thick packet.

The old lady wrote in a small, crabbed hand which made Clare glad she had refrained from crossing her lines. Still, she had needed several pages to apprise him of the situation as it now stood. Beginning by telling him she knew everything—(heavily underscored)—and was completely on his side and Diana's, she proceeded to say that she considered it imperative he make haste to return to town.

"Do not, my dear Clare, refine too much on your mother's behavior," she wrote. "I don't know why she did what she did, but women often take these little crotchets. The best thing to do is ignore her. I, myself, now I am well again, will be very busy you may be sure, nipping any more gossip in the bud. Perhaps I'll even threaten legal action for slander. That should quiet even the most inveterate tattlers.

"But I am sorry I must inform you Diana is planning to leave London. All this has upset her more than I thought possible, and where before she was hot for revenge, now, after learning the identity of the person who wronged her, she wants only to withdraw from society. I don't see how I can hold her in check for very much longer, although I have prevailed on her to remain till Tuesday next, by imploring her not to go before my birthday. That event I have always celebrated in September, and never did I think I would willingly add another year to an already fearsome total, a moment before I had to. However, in this case I could not tell the truth and shame the devil. Ha!"

The duke was beginning to think Lady Michaels more than a little long-winded as he took up yet another sheet covered with her tiny handwriting.

This page was much more interesting, and his face began to lose its heavy frown as he read.

"I believe I have found a solution to your problem with the beauteous Lady C.—and a method to deliver you from what we are all agreed is a most irksome obligation. I may be mistaken, however; therefore it is most important that I speak to you. The answer came to me as I lay in bed recovering from a rheumatic attack, for I have been going over and over everything I knew about the lady, hoping to discover something that might be exploited. I shall be so disappointed if you tell me what I plan won't succeed, but I say no more! This is much too delicate"—(once again, heavily underscored)—"a matter to commit to paper. Do make haste, dear sir, to return to town, and do me the honor of attending me as soon as you arrive. I'll see to it that Diana is not at home if you will give me some idea of the time you might come to me."

She had signed the letter with all the flourishes and compliments of an earlier day, but the duke did not bother to read them. He was already at the library door, shouting for his valet, and ordering his carriage to be brought around.

He was back in town as fast as his fastest team could get him there. Once arrived, he stopped only to remove his hat and driving gloves before he wrote a short note to Lady Michaels, telling her that if it would be convenient, he would call on her the following morning at eleven. A footman was sent running to deliver his message.

As he prepared to go up to his rooms to change his clothes and wash off the road dust, his mother returned home. She was accompanied by Lady Emily whose face lit up in welcome before it returned to an expression of profound dismay.

"Dearest Clare," the dowager exclaimed in her faded voice. "But why had we no warning of your arrival? It was not at all kind of you, for now it is almost too late to request Cornelia join us for dinner. I shall do my best, however, you naughty boy, for I know how you must be longing to see her."

As she came to him, holding up her face for his kiss, the duke thought rather cynically that his mother, as always, was determined to see the world through rose-colored glasses of her own choosing. She was equally determined to make sure everyone else shared her view. For a moment, he stared down at her, then he sighed and kissed her.

"Don't trouble yourself, Mother. I've no intention of seeing Cornelia tonight."

The dowager frowned and clasped her hands to her heart. "Dear Clare, what can you mean? Are you so very tired from your journey?"

"We shall dine *en famille* this evening, Mother. There is a matter of great importance I wish to discuss with you and Emily. And now, you must excuse me. I've only this moment arrived and must change."

As he took the stairs, two at a time, he said over his shoulder, "Join me in the library in half an hour, Em. I've news."

The dowager wrung her hands, not best pleased with this development, but when she turned to discuss it with her daughter, it was to find she too had disappeared. Sighing at her children's behavior, she allowed herself to be helped upstairs by two footmen, and lay down to rest until it should be time to dress for dinner.

When Emily came to the library, she found her brother before her. His kiss for her was much warmer than it had been for their mother, and after she insisted on apologizing for the lady's terrible crime, he shook her lightly.

"Here now, Em, it wasn't *your* fault," he said. "As head of the family I'll attend to Mother. But before we bring all this out in the open I wanted to ask you if she really does have a weak heart? Or are her spells, as I'm beginning to suspect, only a means to get her own way?"

Emily accepted the glass of sherry he had poured her as he spoke, smiling as she did so. "At last you begin to see, m'dear. Of course she is excitable, but no need to fear. Have talked to many doctors. Mama coddles herself. Strong as a wire, assure you."

"In that case, Em, I'm afraid I must ask you one more favor."

"Anything, William, know that," his sister replied in her gruff way.

"You may not be so agreeable when you learn I'm banishing dear Mother to the dower house at Clare Court, and I want you to go with her. But don't worry! It will only be until I can find a companion for her, and so relieve you of this onerous burden. I'm ashamed I didn't do it years ago. I've set all in train for your arrival. An army of servants is already cleaning and polishing."

"Won't like it," Emily warned.

"What Mother likes at this point is of no consequence.

She's forfeited any right to have her wishes attended to, to the exclusion of anyone else's, with her tiresome meddling and her slander. Tell her she may remove anything she wishes to keep from the Court. That will keep her occupied."

Lady Emily laughed. "You'll come back to find it gutted!"

"Good," the duke said cordially. "I've no desire to take Diana to that mausoleum in its present state. If Mother doesn't remove those dreary statues, gloomy paintings, and dreadful bric-a-brac, I'll throw 'em out myself."

Later, the family dinner passed pleasantly enough, but when the three Rawlings retired to the drawing room, and the duke confronted his mother, it was just as well no servants were present. The duchess prepared to have a spell of the first water, but before she could get it well underway, she was told such tactics would no longer suffice. The duke poured her a little brandy, ignoring her fluttering hands, her tears, and her impassioned declaration that it was he who would bring ignominy down on the family name. And, she added, if he jilted Cornelia, he could expect his mother to be carried to her grave in a week, dead of shame. She only hoped he would be able to bear the remorse he would feel as a result for the rest of his life.

"As much remorse and shame as I feel now knowing who started the slander about Diana Travis, ma'am?" he asked softly, although his hazel eyes blazed into hers.

The dowager promptly fainted. When Lady Emily at last restored her to consciousness, she was stunned to see her dear son was completely unmoved, so stunned she sat unprotesting while he laid out her future.

"You will leave for the dower house at the Court as soon as possible, Mother," he said in a voice that permitted no opposition. "There can be no thought of having you live at the Court after the way you have treated Miss Travis. And don't worry. I'm sure Cornelia will be brought of her own free will to jilt me. I don't really care one way or the other, however. My credit is good enough with the world to ride out this storm."

The dowager would have spoken then, her face piteous, but he raised a hand to forestall her. "No, enough," he said and stalked from the room.

"But . . . but Clare, *wait,*" his mother wailed as the door closed behind him. "I was only trying to help you, dearest boy!"

"Not a boy. Doesn't want your help. Leave him alone," Lady Emily told her. The dowager resorted to a flood of tears, but she found her daughter oddly unsympathetic.

The next morning when William Rawlings had breakfast with his sister, he learned that although the dowager had passed a sleepless night and was still inclined to tears, she had taken no harm from his ultimatum. Indeed, she appeared resigned to her banishment, although Emily thought it would take at least a week before she was ready to leave London.

"No hurryin' her, William. Mama's not like you and me, able to pack in an hour. Let her be. She'll not come to any mischief. I'll keep my eye on her, and I've canceled all her engagements."

The duke was forced to agree to the delay, but he charged his sister with keeping his mother and Lady Cornelia apart until he had a chance to see his betrothed himself. He rose then, for he had received a note from Lady Michaels agreeing to his morning visit and he was anxious to be on his way.

The elderly lady was all smiles when he was announced, and dismissed her pale, worried-looking companion immediately. Polly shook her head as she left the room, after being admonished by Lady Michaels to bustle about and order wine for the duke.

Until this had been accomplished, the conversation was of necessity light and inconsequential. Lady Michaels did manage to whisper that Diana had gone out with Lord Evans. "I had to tell him why, sir, so he does not bring her back too soon. The dear boy! He's been the greatest help to us, you know."

But when the butler bowed himself away and closed the drawing room doors, Lady Michaels lost all her customary loquaciousness. She hemmed and hawed, started a sentence only to disregard it after a few words, and outside of a few embarrassed peeks at the duke, seemed to find it difficult to look at him directly.

"But m'lady, what is this all about?" a mystified Duke of Clare was forced to ask at last.

He was surprised to see a blush on her wrinkled cheeks. "Very well," she said at last. "But before I begin, I must ask you to remember I'm old enough to be your grandmother, isn't that so?"

"Even without this extra birthday you have planned," he agreed, trying to put her at her ease.

"Without several of them! As a matter of fact, I knew both your grandmothers. Louisa Rawlings especially was a game 'un, always ready for a frolic and never a mealy word in her mouth. *She'd* understand what I'm about to tell you . . ."

"As I shall try to do, m'lady," he prompted. "Come, it can't be as bad as all that! What do you have to tell me?"

Thus appealed to directly, Lady Michaels took a deep breath and plunged in. "It has occurred to me, Clare, from my observations of Lady Cornelia, that although she is very beautiful in face and form, she is not of a warm, passionate disposition."

She paused as if she expected the duke to reply, but he was so stunned at the direction the conversation had taken, he could only nod.

"You see, I've been observing her most carefully, first at Vauxhall and then at various parties with you. Never once did I see her hanging on your arm, or smiling at you in that special way women have when they . . . when they want a man in their bed. In short, I think the lady cold rather than amorous. Am I correct?"

She sat forward on the edge of her seat, her head tilted to one side in inquiry as she waited for his answer.

"You have it right, ma'am," the duke managed to reply. "In fact, before we were engaged, I named her the Sensuous Ice Maiden. She is certainly voluptuous, but I can feel her steeling herself to endure my kiss, and when I caress her, she becomes almost rigid."

He paused, afraid he must have shocked the old dear. To his surprise, Lady Michaels's wrinkled face was wreathed in smiles and she bounced up and down on the sofa she occupied.

"What a charming marriage you were about to embark on, sir. But never mind that! It is capital—capital! In fact, it couldn't be better. Because I have the solution. But before I tell you of it, I think I'll join you in a glass of wine. In a few moments, you see, I am sure we'll be drinking to your freedom!"

When the duke handed her a brimming glass, she waved him back to his seat again. "Now, Clare," she said, her voice brisk. "Here is what you must do. Since the lady is not at all pleased by your lovemaking—but you must not take that personally, dear boy," she interjected in a different tone. "Daresay she'd be cold to anyone!—what you must do is make love to her without delay. Crush her in your arms, kiss her passionately, fondle her!

Tell her you must marry her at once for you can no longer wait to possess her. You might even leer if you can contrive it, and, oh yes! Announce that you plan to have at least a dozen children and can hardly wait to begin siring 'em! *That* should do it, for no one as conceited as Lady Cornelia wants to have her figger ruined by endless pregnancy.

"Why on *earth* are you laughing, sir?"

The duke had put down his glass and broken into uncontrollable mirth. When he could finally do so, he murmured, "Oh, surely a half dozen little Rawlings will suffice, m'lady?" but that only set him off again. In a moment, Lady Michaels joined him, for although her plan was well-reasoned, still it was ludicrous planning to frighten a woman away by loving her too often.

The two parted in perfect accord after sharing another glass of wine. Lady Michaels gave the duke all the news of Diana he had longed to hear, and he promised to let her know immediately how her stratagems had worked.

As he kissed her hand in parting and told her he would be eternally grateful to her for her help, Lady Michaels reached up to give him a hug. "The woman's a fool, not to want you, Clare," she whispered. "I wish I were fifty years younger, myself. Give Di a rival, I would!"

William Rawlings went home smiling. After putting his sister in the picture, he asked her to write Cornelia and beg her to call that afternoon at three.

"Take Mother for a drive then, Em. I don't want Lady Cornelia forewarned. We're employing shock tactics here, and the element of surprise, you know . . ."

"Think you're disgraceful, William. And who would have thought it of Lady Michaels? Still, wish you the best of luck. Lady C. deserves it."

And so, when Lady Cornelia was ushered into the

drawing room that afternoon, it was not to find a distraught future sister-in-law, but the Duke of Clare instead. He barely waited for the butler to withdraw before he came to her and pulled her into his arms to kiss her with all the passion he could muster.

"Clare, if you please!" the lady said, trying to appear calm when she was allowed to speak at last. "Whatever do you mean by it?"

"But my beautiful one, how can I help it when I've been away from you so long? I was solitary at the Court; my lonely nights troubled with visions of a moment like this. This and so much more. Ah, if I were to tell you of my dreams, you would blush! But this is why I had Em write to you as she did, for I wanted to surprise you. How voluptuous you are! More voluptuous than I remembered."

Cornelia tried to smile, but the duke who had slid her cape from her shoulders, the better to admire her figure clad in fawn lutestring, was staring at her with such blatant hunger she was shocked. Before she could move or protest, he drew her close again. After subjecting her to another searing kiss he began to slide her gown from her shoulders. Cornelia gave a little scream as she pulled away, in her haste leaving a handful of ribbon trim in his possession.

"Stop this at once, Clare!" she panted, very close to hysteria now. "How dare you treat me like some little light-skirt? I'll thank you to remember I'm your future bride!"

"But how do you think brides are treated, my dear?" the duke asked, as she pulled her gown up, much flushed. "Why, they are loved over and over, morning, noon, and night."

"In the morning?" Cornelia whispered, hands to her throat. "*When it is daylight?* No, never!"

"You must never say 'never' to me, Cornelia, and I'll decide the time and place. I'm a very virile man, you know. Indeed, I've found it difficult to give you this time you say you need to become 'accustomed.' Now I'm tired of waiting. You'll soon want me as much as I want you, my sweet. I don't mean to boast, but I've been told I'm a fantastic lover. Assure you, I rarely, er, tire. Come, the wedding will take place in three weeks. I insist on it. And when we go on our wedding journey to Scotland—"

"But I wanted to go to Paris!" Cornelia wailed.

"Scotland," Clare said firmly. "There won't be so many—hm—distractions. I've never cared that much for fishing or hunting stags, and what else is there to do there? Allows us plenty of time to make love, over and over again."

Clare paused, sure she must suspect what he was about, he was laying it on so thick. He warned himself not to get carried away, although he felt he was just beginning to get warmed up for the role he was playing. When he saw Cornelia only looked distraught, twisting her hands and shaking her head in horror at the program he had outlined, he made bold to continue.

"You have to admit I've been very patient, Cornelia. Oh, by the way, I think we should plan to live in Scotland secluded for at least six weeks."

She stared at his powerful, hard body, those determined eyes, his strong hands, and she shuddered.

Although she had not asked, he explained kindly, "The reason I wish to remain that long, dear wife-to-be, is to make sure by that time, and with the program I have in mind, you'll be with child." Here Clare leered at her suggestively as he wondered if he had ever had an ancestor who trod the boards. Acting seemed to come to him so naturally.

"With child?" she echoed, dropping her reticule in her distress.

"Why, yes, the heir to the dukedom, of course. But you are not to worry if we're not successful at first. We can easily remain another month or so. And you must not fret, my dear, if the first child is a girl. My mother had three daughters before me, y'know. And since I plan at least half a dozen children, one or more of them will surely be a boy."

"A half dozen?" Cornelia managed to wail. "No, no!"

Clare came to her to grasp her arms and deliver what he sincerely hoped would be the coup de grâce. "But of course, Cornelia. I'm very fond of children, and you are so strong and healthy. I'm sure you'll manage childbirth easily. Indeed, your excellent health and broad hips were part of the reason I chose you for my wife. It's very important for a duke to marry a good breeder."

"Well, you'll not marry me, you horrible, disgusting *animal*!" she gasped as she twisted out of his grasp. "I'm not a brood mare! And how dare you say I have broad hips? How *dare* you?"

As she spoke she removed her betrothal ring and flung it at his head. It caught him above the right eyebrow, and he could tell from the string and trickle of blood that he would have a deep cut there. A cut he told himself he would be as proud of as any wound received in battle. He hoped Diana would agree.

Cornelia scooped up her reticule and collected her cape, mumbling to herself. As she reached the door, he said in a completely different tone of voice, "Trust me to have the announcement of the termination of our betrothal sent to all the papers at once."

She turned to stare at him, stunned.

"Oh, yes, my *very* clever lady. I've had it written out for some time. I suppose as a gentleman I must wish you well, but may I also express my sincere sympathy for your future husband—whomever he may be, poor devil?"

He bowed slightly and he did not smile. Cornelia suspected that somehow he had found out everything, and she turned to leave as quickly as she could.

"One more thing," that harsh voice said, holding her there with one hand on the doorknob. "If there is any more slander about Diana Travis or about me, I shall know the source. Be sure I shall bring a solicitor with me when I come and call on you. You've been warned. I suggest you begin immediately to let it be known that you were forced to cry off when you discovered we did not suit. I won't contradict you. Unless I have to, that is. Good afternoon."

After Cornelia had escaped at last, the duke sat down in the nearest chair to put his handkerchief to his forehead and utter a silent but heartfelt sigh of relief.

By the time he had written an exultant letter to Lady Michaels, telling her of his success, and sent the necessary notice to the newspapers, William Rawlings felt he had done more than a good day's work.

In his letter, he asked Lady Michaels to say nothing since he wanted to be the first to tell Diana the good news. And although he would have liked to do everything properly, traveling to Crompton Abbey to ask Mr. Travis for her hand, with the announcement about to appear and all London soon to be buzzing with the news, he would have to forgo that formality.

He was smiling as he sealed his letter, for he knew very

well that it was not so much regret that he could not go about things properly, as it was simply he could not wait a moment longer than he had to to take Diana in his arms again.

12

The following morning, the duke was up and dressed at an hour that generally he would have castigated as fit only for milkmaids. He had his breakfast, attended to some correspondence in what his secretary considered an abstracted way, and told his sister to have a good ride when she left for an early morning canter in the park. Lady Emily grinned as she wished him good fortune, for he had announced his hopefully short-term freedom at dinner the previous evening.

At last he felt the hour late enough to make a morning call on a lady, although he hoped Diana still kept country hours. He was in the hall pulling on his gloves while a footman held his hat and cane at the ready, when the dowager drifted down the stairs to intercept him. She was very pale this morning, for her son's announcement at dinner had sunk her into deep despair and she had spent another restless night. The duke noticed eyes puffy from weeping, and hands that continually twisted a handkerchief, and he steeled himself.

"Dearest son," she began, then gave a heartrending sigh. "I do beg you, Clare, to reconsider while there is still time. But we cannot talk here in the hall. Please come with me to the library."

The duke frowned even as he reminded himself he

must be gentle. She was still his mother, after all. "I cannot tarry, Mother. My errand is much too important," he said. "Besides, nothing you could say could change my mind. Excuse me."

Taking his hat and cane from the footman, he left the house. In his pocket he carried the diamond and emerald betrothal ring of the Rawlings. He wondered if he should stop along the way and purchase the largest bouquet of roses he could carry. But so intent was he on his destination, he decided not to take the time. He did not even hear the greeting called to him from an acquaintance as he hurried along.

Lady Michaels did not keep him waiting. As the butler bowed him into the drawing room, she instructed that servant to ask Miss Diana to join her as soon as possible, but on no account to mention they were entertaining a visitor.

"We'll surprise her, dear boy! How glad I am to see you, but never fear. I am going away immediately so you may see Diana alone," she told him, her eyes twinkling. "Mind you now, I want to hear how it all went as soon as possible."

It was only a few minutes after she left the room that Diana slipped inside the door. To William Rawlings, however, who had spent the time pacing up and down, it seemed an age.

Diana was wearing a simple morning gown of white, and she looked so lovely standing in the doorway with her hands clasped to her heart in surprise, the duke's own heart began to beat erratically.

"Dearest Di, at last," he said as he came toward her to lead her unresisting to a brocaded loveseat. Diana, who had yet to utter a word, stared at him, her face white with shock.

When Lady Michaels had reported to the duke that

Diana was so upset she only wanted to retire to Eastham, she had not been entirely correct. It was true her great-niece had been sunk in depression for a few days after learning it was Clare's own mother who had started the rumors. But then her temper got the best of her again and she became determined to make the entire Rawlings family pay for ruining her reputation and causing her such unhappiness. How she was to do this she did not know, although Lord Evans had let slip that Clare had returned to London when the two had been strolling in the park the previous morning. Pierpont Evans liked Diana and he thought it very hard she should be treated like a pariah. But he could tell, even though she pretended nothing was wrong, that she was very much aware of the whispers and stares, the pointed fingers and titters from those who did not know as yet the whole story was a lie. Lord Evans wished he might have told Diana that Clare was about to break his engagement with La Cornelia, but since both the duke and Lady Michaels had his promise to remain silent, there was nothing he could do except hope Clare made all right as soon as possible.

Now, Diana took a deep breath and clasped her hands in her lap to hide their trembling. "I was not aware you had called or I would not have come down, sir. But perhaps the butler summoned me by mistake?"

The duke, about to take the seat beside her and take her in his arms as well, was stopped by the coldness in her voice. "My dear Diana, how icy you are!"

"There is nothing you and I could possibly have to discuss, sir," she said, about to get to her feet and leave him.

Unbidden, the duke sat down and grasped her arms to keep her beside him. "Now what is all this about, my girl?" he asked. "Nothing to discuss? We've a lifetime of things to discuss!"

"I must say I'm surprised you came, never mind remain here alone with me, Your Grace," Diana told him, suddenly voluble. "Surely that is to risk society's damnation, even for a man like you. You see, while you've been out of town, I've acquired a most unsavory reputation." Her voice was more normal now, although he could hear undertones of her anger as she went on, "Oh yes, my name has been bandied far and wide as a wanton. It is even general knowledge I make a practice of spending the night with various gentlemen. But perhaps you came to arrange a similar assignation? Of course! How stupid of me not to—oh!"

She gasped with pain as he gripped her arms tightly. "Don't ever, *ever* say anything like that again!" he told her. "I will not have you insulting yourself that way!"

"You are hurting me," she managed to get out, frightened of the light she could see deep in his eyes. She was released at once.

Diana ignored her aching arms. She would not rub them before him. "In any case," she went on, "it was most unwise for you to call here. But you must not fear I will mention your visit for I am going home to Eastham. Home, where people behave decently, and do not ruin you for amusement or spite. Home, where there are no rakes to make love to you and tell you lies."

Her voice broke a little under her sarcasm, and she turned her head away as the duke stared at her.

"I forgot you don't know yet," he began, his voice carefully controlled. He had seen the fear in her eyes when she looked at him and he was ashamed of himself. The last thing he wanted to do in the world was frighten her.

"My engagement to the devious Lady Cornelia is at an end. The announcement of its demise will appear in the next edition of the journals. I am free now. I would not have come to you otherwise."

Diana turned to stare at him, hope dawning in her eyes. Then her expression changed and she shrugged. "What difference does that make now? After the scandal and what I have discovered—no, I'm for Crompton Abbey."

"I see," the duke said, not even trying to convince her to change her mind, much to her dismay. "You will, however, have the kindness to hear me out."

Gently he took her hands in his and said, "I came here to ask you to marry me. If you remember, some months ago I told you you'd be my duchess. I was not lying then. I am not lying now, and I have not changed my mind. Nothing could make me do that, certainly not some society gossip that is as silly as it is untrue. I love you, Diana. I love you more than I believed I could love anyone. And somehow I sense you love me in return—"

"Whatever I feel does not matter," she cried, tearing her hands from his and drawing back, away from his disturbing nearness. "I have other reasons, you see . . . reasons that make it impossible for me to contemplate such a step. You must believe me, Clare! You and I will never marry, not now."

"You do see you must tell me why not, don't you, my dear?" he said calmly. "I'll never believe it, otherwise."

She cast about in her mind for something to tell him for she did not think she could bear to be the one who revealed his mother's part. "Well, there is Sir Percy Nottingham," she got out finally.

The duke's brows rose. "Sir Percy? What has he to say to anything?"

"He was the one who told me of the gossip. I might never have discovered it for my great-aunt has been ill, and all I could do was wonder why people were treating me badly. But Sir Percy was so kind as to enlighten me when he kidnapped me one afternoon for what I believe all the worst gothic tales call 'his own nefarious purposes.' "

"He dared *touch* you?" Clare demanded, his face black with anger again.

"Not for long," Diana hurried to assure him. "I boxed his ears, kicked him hard, and gave him a bloody nose."

"Is that all? Still, that would tend to make it clear to even the most obtuse gentleman you did not care for his advances. But tell me, why is any of this a reason to prevent us marrying?"

"Well, no doubt he'll brag about his conquest, even though there never was one," Diana said, not looking at the duke now.

"Come, come, I think we may disregard Sir Percy. He'll never dare mention your name for he knows what I would do to him if he so forgot himself. No, I think it is time you told me the *real* reason. The one you haven't disclosed as yet. I'm prepared to wait you know. I've all day."

Diana put her hands to her face for a moment, then she took a deep breath. "Very well, if you insist. I did not want to distress you, but I see there is no other way. The person who started the gossip about me was your own mother. Lord Evans found her out. There can be no mistake. So you see how impossible marriage between us is now. How could I even contemplate such a thing knowing what she has done; how much she must hate me? I don't think I could forgive her even if she begged me to. No, I won't marry you, and I . . . I wish you would go away!"

She saw the duke's face stiffen, and for the first time noticed the small livid cut over his right eyebrow. It made him look like a devil, but his voice when he spoke was even.

"You will do me the kindness to accept my most profound apologies for my mother's behavior, Miss Travis. What she did was inexcusable, and she shall pay for it. May I also say how sorry I am her actions make it impossible for you to have me to husband, even though I understand your reasons, and must accept them, no matter how unhappy it makes me. You shall have your revenge. I shall insist my mother apologize to you in person—"

Suddenly he rose and almost ran to the door. Diana watched him, her heart sinking. She had done what she planned and driven him away forever. It was strange that the revenge that should have tasted so sweet, made her want to cry instead. She got up to go to him, holding out her hands as he opened the door and surprised Lady Michaels's butler, lingering in the hall outside.

"I am sure this has been most edifying for you," Clare snapped. "But now I must ask you to cease eavesdropping and have Miss Travis's maid bring her cloak down at once. She is going out."

He slammed the door in the butler's red face and came back to take Diana's arm. She tried to resist, but he was having none of that.

"Go out? Where?" she said, startled by this order. "Are you mad? You can see I'm not dressed for the street. Dear God, there will be more talk, more gossip, as if London has not had enough to say about me these past few weeks!"

"Eventually you'll learn how little of what the ton says matters to me. And since this affair has been a disaster of mistakes from start to finish, why change its direction now? But if you thought I would calmly accept your dismissal and walk away from you before my mother had tendered her apologies in person, you mistake my character."

Diana tugged to free her arm again, and he put his other hand over hers. "Stop that! You'll go with me if I have to drag you there, kicking and screaming the entire length of the streets. Do your worst! Even that will not deter me!"

"I think you're insane," Diana panted, and the duke laughed at her, a bitter, mocking laugh.

"Oh, quite mad, my dear, at least as far as you are concerned. I've known it this age."

There was a timid knock on the door, and Betty came in to curtsy, her eyes wide and her hands shaking as she held out Diana's bonnet and a light cloak. "Beggin' yer pardon, miss," she whispered, "an' I know I shouldn't speak up, but what would your mother an' father say? Goin' out with him like this, an' not *reelly* dressed, even if he is a *dook*? Why, you still have your house slippers on."

"Quiet!" the duke thundered, his face dark as he dropped the cloak over Diana's shoulders and put on her bonnet. She reached up automatically to straighten it for he had merely crammed it on her black hair and she was sure she must look a perfect fright with the large brim tipping over one eye and the ribbons and flowers with which it was trimmed going every which way.

Before she could set it right, the duke grasped her arm again and hustled her through the front hall to the door. The butler opened it, redeeming himself by bowing with aplomb, as if Miss Travis was so eccentric she always left home in this manner. Diana could hear Betty's whimpers behind her, but then Clare took her down the steps, one strong arm around her waist. She felt as if her feet never touched the ground.

"How can you do this?" she wailed, trying to fasten the ties of her cloak so she would not lose it in the speed of their passage.

"You had better save your breath, Miss Travis," he said as he pushed between two elderly dowagers deep in conversation. "I'm in a hurry."

"Well!" said one lady, tottering to a lamppost for support.

" 'Pon my soul," replied her companion, grasping the palings near her and dropping her parcels.

"Your pardon, ladies," Clare said, not abating his pace one iota.

Diana tried to appear easy. She told herself the reason she didn't ask the ladies for help was because she was afraid Clare would throttle her if she dared. He certainly looked angry enough to do so. Suddenly she saw Pierpont Evans and another gentleman coming toward them, and her heart leapt. Surely Lord Evans would help her escape from this madman—discreetly, too.

Lord Evans made them an elegant leg, slow to notice Clare had forgotten to wear a hat this morning. Then he saw he had neglected to bring his gloves and cane along, and the generally neat and stylish Miss Travis wore only a simple gown covered by a cloak that was slipping from her shoulders. Her bonnet was askew as well.

"Going for a walk, m'dears?" he asked, staring at them in bewilderment.

"Lord Evans, save me!" Diana hissed, trying to keep the stranger from hearing.

"Save you?" he echoed in a loud voice. "From what?"

The gentleman with him raised his quizzing glass to stare. "That you, Clare?" he asked. "What's to do?"

"Out of my way, both of you," the duke said, pushing past them as he hurried Diana along.

"For heaven's sake, Lord Evans, help me," Diana called over her shoulder as her bonnet fell to the flags. "The duke is kidnapping me!"

"Never say so," the strange gentleman sputtered, picking up the charming, bedecked bonnet and staring at it in amazement. "Here now, Clare, this won't do, dear boy! Bad ton! And the young lady's hat—"

"Why don't we all retire to a quiet spot to discuss it, Clare?" Pierpont Evans added. "Perhaps a glass of wine will cool your fever, or—"

But Diana heard no more, for the duke was whisking her around the corner of Eaton Square. She stole a quick glance at his dark face and saw his lips were compressed with anger, those hazel eyes blazing.

"I think I hate you!" she told him, seeing Mrs. Hawley stop dead across the square to point out this unusual twosome to her three companions. "There is Mrs. Hawley! Now this will be all over London in a matter of minutes!"

"And what do you care?" the duke asked as he avoided one liveried footman running an errand for his master, and another walking m'lady's pug. "You are for Crompton Abbey, aren't you?"

The pug yapped at them both. Suddenly one of Diana's slippers fell off, to the delight of the little dog. It made a rush to capture and shake it. "Stop—my slipper!" Diana exclaimed, digging in her heels and trying to halt the duke's impetuous progress. For a moment, he paused, but it was only to sweep her up in his arms before he continued his march. Over his arm, Diana saw Mrs. Hawley staring after them, eyes big with shock, and she pounded the duke's chest with her fists. "I'll never forgive you for this, Clare, never, do you hear me?"

The duke did not reply as he went up the steps of Clare House and pounded on the front door. It was opened almost at once by his butler. Many times in his long career, that servant had had to school his features to indifference, but although not a muscle in his face betrayed him, surely he had never been so sorely tested before.

"Your Grace, Miss Travis," he said, bowing and holding the door wide so they might enter. He frowned at one of the footmen whose mouth had dropped open in amazement. The duke set Diana on her feet, and she tried to smooth her windblown hair. The old nursery rhyme about "one shoe off and one shoe on," echoed in her head as the duke took her arm and marched her toward his library. "Tell my mother I wish to see her at once, Hibbert."

The butler coughed. "I beg your pardon, Your Grace. The dowager is not here."

The duke paused. He had not expected this, for he had been sure he would find his mother deep in one of her spells after their conversation that morning.

"Not here? Where has she gone?"

"She went out right after you left, sir, and I heard her instruct the coachman to take her to Lady Stafford's."

Clare frowned. Would the woman never give up? "We'll wait for her in the library. See that we're not disturbed, and bring the dowager to me as soon as she enters the house."

"Very good, Your Grace," the butler murmured. Clare did not hear him. He was slamming the library doors behind him and his captive.

He released Diana and bowed to her. "I apologize for the delay, Miss Travis, but as soon as my mother arrives, you shall have your apology, and whatever other revenge you wish to exact."

Diana sank down into a leather armchair, completely at

a loss. The duke's voice had been cold and formal. He seemed to have taken her at her word and given up trying to make her promise to marry him. But why wouldn't he? she asked herself. I told him I wouldn't more than once. And I told him I'd never forgive him, and just a few minutes ago, I even said I hated him! Oh, *why* did I do that? She swore at herself because now she knew that none of this mattered the least little bit. Not his mother's dislike, or her slander—not even what the haut ton would say. It didn't even matter that Clare was autocratic and maddening and would probably lead her a merry dance for the rest of her life. He was the only man she wanted, and she knew she'd be all kind of fool to let him go.

She took a deep breath and looked straight into those haunting eyes as she said in a small voice, "But I find I don't want revenge on her, Clare. Not now. To be truthful, I only want . . ."

The duke stared at her as her voice died away. His hazel eyes were intent and he cocked his head to one side in polite interest. For a moment, Diana's courage faltered.

"Yes, Miss Travis? I shall of course make it a primary concern of mine, as a way of making amends, to see your wishes are satisfied. You want, Miss Travis . . . ?"

Suddenly Diana's quick temper exploded. "Will you stop calling me 'Miss Travis' in that stupid, formal way? Especially after what you have just done, dragging me through the streets like a sack of meal? And stop asking me what I want when you must know very well that what I want is . . ."

Clare folded his arms across his chest, but he made no move to approach her, and his face gave nothing away of his feelings.

"Perhaps I want to hear you say it out loud, beauty, so this time there can be no mistake," he said softly.

For a moment there was complete silence, and Diana swallowed hard. "I want what you have led me to believe you want, too," she whispered.

"Cowardly, and I never thought it of you," he told her, not taking his eyes from her pale face.

Thus challenged, she rose and strode up to him. "Very well, if you will insist I do it! My mother would be horrified to see me making love to you, you shameless man! Forget what I said this morning, for I lied. What I *want,* what I have *always* wanted, and always *will* want, is you! But—"

She was allowed to say no more, for the duke, abandoning his carefully controlled pose, swept her into his arms and kissed her.

As those arms tightened around her and his lips claimed hers, Diana gave herself up to the sensation of falling he was able to bring her to that she had known so few times before now. Her arms went around him in turn, and she responded to him as she had never dared before. It was a very long time before the duke raised his head and stared down at her half-closed eyes and moist, parted lips while he watched the roses coming and going in her cheeks. He could not resist kissing her again before he whispered, "And you shall have me, dear love, as I shall have you. Forever. Never mind my mother. She's removing to the dower house immediately, and you won't even have to meet her again if you don't care to. As for the ton, they'll follow my lead. I'm sure what we did this morning and the news of our betrothal will be a seven-day wonder, but what do we care? Soon there'll be a new on dit to set all the old tabbys gossiping. Tell me you don't mind."

His hand caressed her throat down to the neck of her gown and Diana smiled at him. "How can I cry propriety after what I've just done? As for the dowager, of course we must meet now we are family. I'll even try not to mind when she calls me 'Duchess . . . Duchess?'. . . "

She would have continued but he took her face between his hands and kissed her laughing mouth. "I want you as soon as possible," he muttered harshly, before he buried his face in her cloud of midnight-black hair.

"Gretna, sir?" Diana asked demurely.

"Certainly not." He left her abruptly and walked to the fireplace to lean against the mantel, running his hands through his hair in an abstracted way. For a moment, Diana was bewildered, but then she swaggered up to him, her chin jutting out aggressively as she said, " 'Ere now, wot's all this then? No Gretna? Let me tell you, me foine duke, *Hi'm* not to be 'ad wiffout me marriage lines!"

She scowled at him hands on hips, and his harsh expression broke into curves of laughter.

"Dearest Di, you witch! How can I resist you, especially with your hair down your back and only one shoe on? I only meant no Gretna for you, beauty! Westminster Abbey, or perhaps St. Paul's, but nothing less for the future Duchess of Clare. But how to do it quickly?"

Diana saw such naked longing for her in his eyes that she put her arms around him and buried her face in his cravat, humbled by the depths of his feelings.

"We'll put my great-aunt onto it, Will. Give her twenty-four hours, my darling, and you'll be surprised." Then she burrowed closer and whispered, "How lowering it is to discover I'm the shameless hussy society named me after all! Because, you see, I find I can't wait for you, either."

She was surprised when he put her aside to walk to the library door. "Will?" she asked. "But what is it? Where are you going?"

He turned and smiled at her, and she melted. "I'm not going anywhere except to tell Hibbert it won't be necessary for him to bring my mother in here as soon as she returns. Then I'm going to lock this door so we'll be assured of complete privacy. Somehow I'm sure you won't mind waiting for her apology, will you, love? Especially since we're going to be very busy with—mm—more important things?

"Why, my dearest Di, I never realized how adorable you'd look, blushing!"

Epilogue

A mere two weeks later, William John St. Denis Rawlings, the Duke of Clare, the Earl of Brecken, and the Lord of Hentings and Stark, took as his bride Miss Diana Travis of Crompton Abbey, Eastham. Everyone agreed the bride was stunning in her white lace gown, a matching veil covering her dark hair. That veil was crowned with a tiara of diamonds and emeralds, the groom's gift.

Certainly the wedding was the perfect ending to a brilliant season's most stormy courtship, and although the cathedral was crowded, it came as no surprise to anyone that Lady Cornelia had retired to the country and did not attend. Quite a few guests remarked the absence of the dowager duchess as well, and said what a shame it was the lady had succumbed to another heart spell and thus was unable to see her handsome son take as his bride such a radiant young lady.

As the organ swelled in the recessional, and the newly married pair turned to walk back down the aisle, several elderly ladies wiped away tears. The new duchess held out her hand, and the duke, before tucking it in his arm, raised it to his lips in tribute. But no one heard Diana whisper,

" 'Here's my hand,' " nor the duke reply as he finished the quotation, " 'And mine, with my heart in't.' "

And what happened to everyone after the wedding? The dowager duchess, with a new companion and nurse began to travel the world extensively, from one spa to the next. Lady Emily took up dog breeding at one of the duke's lesser seats and was happy for the first time in her life. Roger Maitland married a lovely girl from his home county who had been right under his nose, unheeded for years. As for Cornelia, she became the wife of General Lord Haven. He was an extremely wealthy, retired gentleman of eighty years of age. It was said he adored her.

And a year later, Lady Michaels stood beaming as she held the future Duke of Clare for his christening at St. Paul's, but it was her faithful companion who had the last word. As everyone turned from the baptismal font, and the duke bent to kiss his wife, Polly leaned over to whisper to the old lady, "Well done, ma'am! I can hear those Roman candles and salutes going off still!"

SIGNET REGENCY ROMANCE

WHEN LOVE CONQUERS ALL

☐ **ROGUE'S DELIGHT by Elizabeth Jackson.** The handsome and heartless Viscount Everly needed a wife for the sake of show. So how could an impoverished orphan like Miss Susan Winston say no? But playing the part of Lord Everly's pawn was one thing—and becoming a plaything of passion was another. (182774—$3.99)

☐ **LORD CAREW'S BRIDE by Mary Balogh.** When the beautiful Samantha Newman is faced with a marriage proposal and new feelings that have been stirred by the charming Marquess of Carew, she must decide if she can resist her strong attraction to the Earl of Rushford, the notorious libertine who betrayed her six years ago—or ignite the flames of a new passion. (185528—$3.99)

☐ **THE KINDER HEART by Marcy Elias Rothman.** Lady Barbara Worth had good reason to mistrust men. Her own brother left her impoverished while he dissipated their family fortune gambling, wenching, and worse, and her former suitors had abandoned her to solitude. Then, Captain Tarn Maitland thrust himself into her tranquil life. What malevolent motive did this wealthly, handsome, irresistible man—with a dark secret—have in seeking Lady Barbara as his wife? (179226—$3.99)

☐ **THE WILLFUL WIDOW by Evelyn Richardson.** Lady Diana Hatherill had been married once—and once was quite enough—her husband died in the same reckless manner in which he had lived, leaving her with nothing but debts. Lady Diana had no problem bewitching a swarm of suitors while keeping them at bay—until Lord Justin St. Clair arrived on the scene. Marriage was not on his mind, but mischief most certainly was. (178696—$3.99)

*Prices slightly higher in Canada

Buy them at your local bookstore or use this convenient coupon for ordering.

PENGUIN USA
P.O. Box 999 — Dept. #17109
Bergenfield, New Jersey 07621

Please send me the books I have checked above.
I am enclosing $________________ (please add $2.00 to cover postage and handling). Send check or money order (no cash or C.O.D.'s) or charge by Mastercard or VISA (with a $15.00 minimum). Prices and numbers are subject to change without notice.

Card #________________________ Exp. Date ________________
Signature____
Name____
Address____
City ________________ State ____________ Zip Code ____________

For faster service when ordering by credit card call **1-800-253-6476**

Allow a minimum of 4-6 weeks for delivery. This offer is subject to change without notice.

SIGNET REGENCY ROMANCE

NOVELS OF LOVE AND DESIRE

☐ **THE COUNTERFEIT GENTLEMAN by Charlotte Louise Dolan.** Can Miss Bethia Pepperell win the heart of a maddeningly mocking miscreant who comes from lowly origins and makes his living outside the law? (177428—$3.99)

☐ **AN AMIABLE ARRANGEMENT by Barbara Allister.** Miss Lucy Meredith thought she knew what she was doing when she wed Richard Blount over the opposition of her father and her brother. But she was in need of a husband—Richard was in need of a wife, and their union would solve both their problems—or will it? (179420—$3.99)

☐ **THE RAKE AND THE REDHEAD by Emily Hendrickson.** Beautiful Hyacinthe Dancy finds Blase, Lord Norwood, to be the most infuriatingly arrogant man she has ever met and she vows to stay well clear of this man and his legendary charm. . . . But when Lord Norwood sets out to destroy an old village, Hyacinthe places herself in Norwood's path, and finds he has the power to ignite more than her temper. (178556—$3.99)

☐ **ELIZABETH'S GIFT by Donna Davidson.** Elizabeth Wydner knew her own mind—and what she knew about her mind was remarkable. For Elizabeth had the power to read the thoughts of others, no matter how they masked them. She saw into the future as well, spotting lurking dangers and hidden snares. Elizabeth felt herself immune to falsehood and safe from surprise—until she met Nathan Lord Hawksley. (180089—$3.99)

*Prices slightly higher in Canada

Buy them at your local bookstore or use this convenient coupon for ordering.

PENGUIN USA
P.O. Box 999 — Dept. #17109
Bergenfield, New Jersey 07621

Please send me the books I have checked above.
I am enclosing $_______________ (please add $2.00 to cover postage and handling). Send check or money order (no cash or C.O.D.'s) or charge by Mastercard or VISA (with a $15.00 minimum). Prices and numbers are subject to change without notice.

Card #_______________ Exp. Date _______________
Signature_______________
Name_______________
Address_______________
City _______________ State _______________ Zip Code _______________

For faster service when ordering by credit card call **1-800-253-6476**

Allow a minimum of 4-6 weeks for delivery. This offer is subject to change without notice.